MY
SECRET
LIES
WITH
YOU

For Julia, Eliza and Newellie, Mum and Webber and
the holidays we spent together in Ynys, North Wales.
And also for Rosa. You're a star. You know why!

First published in the UK in 2019 by Usborne Publishing Ltd., Usborne House,
83-85 Saffron Hill, London EC1N 8RT, England. www.usborne.com

Copyright © 2019 by Faye Bird

The right of Faye Bird to be identified as the author of this work has been asserted by
her in accordance with the Copyright, Designs and Patents Act, 1988.

Photography: Front cover – © Getty images – Chen Liu / EyeEm

Back cover – © Shutterstock – Jamie Casper

The name Usborne and the devices ♀ ⊕USBORNE are Trade Marks of
Usborne Publishing Ltd.

This is a work of fiction. The characters, incidents, and dialogues are products of the
author's imagination and are not to be construed as real. Any resemblance to actual
events or persons, living or dead, is entirely coincidental.

A CIP catalogue record for this book is available from the British Library.

ISBN 9781474958240 05202/1 JFM MJJASOND/19

Printed in the UK.

FAYE BIRD

MY SECRET LIES WITH YOU

USBORNE

ALYS

When I first saw you all sitting, talking, laughing, by the lifeguard hut on the beach, you all looked so happy. It was kind of intoxicating. I watched you for a little while, and then I kept on watching. I couldn't stop. All I wanted was to have what you all had. And as I watched I only had one thought – I want to be a part of that. *The day we spent together at the lake was one of the best. If I hadn't seen you that day, spent it with you, I'm not sure I would have ever done what I did. So I want to say thank you. And I hope that if you feel what I have done is wrong, you will find a way to forgive me, and if you don't understand why I am doing what I'm doing now, this letter will in some way help you try.*

PART
ONE

THIS
SUMMER

CAIT

FRIDAY

1

Arriving at the cottage felt like arriving at the edge of the world.

"So, we're here," Mum said, getting out of the car. I could smell how different the place was as soon as she opened the door. It was the air. Cows. Or was it just a general farm smell? I wasn't sure. Fresh and not-fresh all at the same time. It hit the inside of my nose and the coolness of it tingled.

Wales.

North Wales.

We were so far away from London now.

I watched Johnny get out of the car, and follow Mum over onto the grass. He stood behind her and wrapped his arms around her belly as they looked on together at the view. An estuary. Sheep. Mountains. I stayed in the car. I didn't care that I'd already been in it for six horribly long hours, relegated to the back like a little kid while Mum and Johnny talked and laughed and forgot I was even there. I mean, occasionally Mum would turn round and smile, pass me a sweet, a chocolate eclair or something, and I'd hate myself for kind of grunting back from under my headphones, because acting like this, feeling like I did, it really wasn't me. It wasn't who I am or the kind of person I wanted to be. It was just that coming on this so-called holiday with Mum and Johnny, out in this middle of nowhere place, was really the last thing in the world I wanted to do. And for some reason, despite all my moods in the week leading up to it, when Mum had suggested it and booked it all at the last minute, she hadn't picked up on the fact that I didn't want to go. And I just hadn't had the heart to tell her.

Mum broke herself free from Johnny's arms and came back to the car, opening the boot.

"Come on, Cait," she said. "Let's get our stuff and open up the cottage. Ours is the one on the left."

I looked over at the cottages – just two of them, sitting very slightly apart on a grassy bank at the edge of the estuary.

I turned back to Mum. She was smiling. She looked really excited to be here. Didn't she get that I'd just spent all of today feeling like a complete spare wheel? Didn't she get that I'd rather be back at home in London with my friends? Didn't she get that the idea of being here for two whole weeks with this…this scenery, this smell, and her and loved-up Johnny was not my idea of a holiday at all? I mean, Mia was in Ibiza and Jade was in Malta. And me? I was in the depths of Snowdonia with my mum and her new boyfriend and it was completely, absolutely, the last place in the world I wanted to be.

"It's cute," Johnny said as we walked into the cottage.

It was small. Tiny, in fact. The three of us couldn't fit in the hall with our bags. I was half in, half out of the front door as Johnny stood at the bottom of the stairs with Mum in between. It was only when Mum moved along a bit, and Johnny shoved his case onto the stairs, that I could completely step inside.

Damp.

That's what I could smell. And the walls, they were painted a gross, buttery yellow. Or had they been white and just turned yellow over the years? I couldn't tell, but they were bumpy and rough to touch. It looked like someone had thrown a handful of rocks into the paint. And I was sure the temperature inside the house had literally dropped three degrees compared to what it felt like outside.

"Nice slate floor," Mum said, shuffling along.

"Local stone," Johnny said. "Tons of it around."

"I'm going to go up and put these bags in our room," Mum said, and as she went up the stairs I literally thought they were going to come away from the wall with all the creaking.

I kicked my bag under the stairs and went through a door opposite into a snug little room with a window seat and a couple of sofas. There was a television on a dark wooden table. It seriously looked like it should have been in some kind of museum. I found the remote and switched it on. I heard sound before a picture appeared; alien voices, garbled words I couldn't make sense of, rushing, clunky, fast, and then I realized – it was Welsh. The programme was in Welsh. I carried on watching as the picture emerged. It looked like a daytime drama or soap. People I didn't recognize, speaking a language I couldn't understand, and yet I wasn't in the heart of some glamorous European city. I was still here in the UK, in a cottage that seemed to have a sub-zero temperature of its own. It was all so much worse than I'd even expected it to be.

"Cait!" I heard Mum calling from upstairs.

"Yeah?" I said, and I switched off the TV and moved from the sitting room back into the hall to follow her voice. I wondered if my hoody was still in the car. I seriously needed to put on another layer.

"Will you bring some more stuff in?" Mum said. "And pop the kettle on while you're down there?"

"Yeah," I said, and I went through the only other door off the hallway and found the kitchen. A set of cabinets, a sink, more yellowing walls, and a tiny little window at the back looking out onto a scrap of grass with a tree and a plastic swing. And beyond that there was a gate that went straight out onto the estuary – the estuary being a whole load of grasses and marsh, and eventually it looked like there was possibly some sand before the water.

I found the kettle and flicked it on, pulling open the nearest cupboard to look for teabags and mugs. I pulled out three and set them on the worktop. Three mugs. Three. Three always used to mean Mum, Dad and me. Not any more. No one tells you that when someone dies, it's the stupid little things – three teabags, three mugs, just the number three – that floor you. Little things that lurk in grief's dark corners and jump out and grab hold of you at the most unexpected times.

Where are you, Dad?

I'd often found myself saying those words over the last eighteen months. Sometimes I'd say them out loud, sometimes just in my head. I'm not sure why. I think it was just the comfort of talking to someone…no, talking to *him*. I knew that if he could see me now, standing here, in this cottage, making tea, he'd have said something like, *Oh, Cait. Not quite the holiday you were hoping for, eh? Come on, give me a hug. We'll make it fun, okay?* And it would always work; whatever he said it always seemed to make things better. He could make everything okay.

"Oh…you're making tea!" Johnny said, coming into the kitchen. "Great."

I nodded and walked quickly over to the fridge.

"Hopefully there'll be some milk in here," I said, opening the door, and sticking my head in, partly so I didn't have to look at Johnny, partly so I didn't have to keep making more conversation. I mean, I knew I needed to make the effort with Johnny, but it was really hard. We had literally nothing in common but Mum.

"Yup, milk, and there's some butter here too," I said walking back to the mugs with the milk.

"Just a drop for me, thanks, Cait," he said, coming to stand next to me, watching me pour and stir. He was really annoying me now. I wished he'd just go away.

"Where's Mum?" I asked. Really for something to say, because the kitchen felt even smaller now, like there was no room to breathe with just me and Johnny in it.

"She's still unpacking. You should take your stuff up. Your room is nice. It's the one at the front. You can get yourself sorted."

I nodded, hating him for telling me what to do, and then I watched him take two mugs and go out the kitchen and back up to Mum.

I looked at my tea, the one left on the side. I didn't want it now. I picked the mug up and sloshed the contents into the sink, watching the steam rise as the brown liquid slinked its way down the plughole. I went back out of the house towards the car to find my hoody and try and shake the chill I could feel against my skin just from being here.

I opened up the car and reached in. My hoody was lying on the back seat. It was mad how much warmer it was being outside the house than in. It was actually ridiculous.

"Hey!"

A voice. I looked to see where it was coming from. I hadn't seen any other signs of life, anyone else around.

"You just arrived?"

A boy was walking towards me now from the road, wearing colours that were way too bright – red shorts and a huge oversized red hoody. I smiled at him, and noticed his black hair and deep olive skin. He kind of exuded warmth in the coolness of this place, and it wasn't just his clothes.

"Yeah," I said. "Just arrived."

"From London?"

I nodded, and noticed how dark his eyes were too. They were so brown they were almost black. "So does everyone who stays here come from London, then?"

"A few," he said. "Getting away from it all."

"Right," I said, nodding.

"You can't get more away from it all than here, I guess," he said.

I nodded. "Yup," I said. He was so right.

"I'm Marko," he said. "I'm in the cottage next door, staying with my dad. I'm here for most of the summer." He pointed to the cottage along from ours.

I nodded again. He was so easy with himself, and so friendly, so familiar with me, I almost thought I was going to blush, but I didn't. Instead I just kept nodding like some kind of idiot.

"And you are?" he said, smiling.

"God, sorry, yes, I'm Cait. We're here for a couple of weeks."

"Great," he said. "Great – Cait…well nice to meet you. If you need anything at all while you're here then just let me know."

"Thanks," I said, and as he started to walk across the gravel in front of the cottages and over to his front door, glancing back at me, I lifted up my hand as if to wave and then stopped myself. What was I doing?

"Listen…" he said, "if you fancy coming to a party, we're having one at the beach tomorrow night. It'll be a good one. You should come."

"Oh, right, okay," I said. "Thanks." I stood there for a moment, wondering what to say or what to do with my face, because I'd been here less than an hour and had managed to get myself invited to a party and I wasn't quite sure how I'd done that. Admittedly I'd been invited by a slightly over-friendly boy who was definitely older than me, dressed predominantly in fire-engine red. But still…

I was pretty sure I wasn't going to go – there was no way I'd be brave enough to just turn up on my own to a beach party with a whole bunch of strangers on a Saturday night but I liked the thought that I'd been asked. I liked it a lot. Maybe this holiday wasn't going to be quite as dead as I'd thought after all.

SATURDAY

2

"We thought we'd go into Harlech this morning. Johnny wants to get a paper and I'd like to wander around the shops, pick up some food," Mum said as she came into the kitchen. She looked ready for the day. So much more ready than me.

I nodded, but I really didn't want to go.

I stood, leaning against the kitchen cupboards, taking in another spoonful of my breakfast cereal really slowly. The milk kind of dribbled down my chin and I wiped it with my pyjama sleeve.

"I wish you'd sit at the table to eat your breakfast, Cait. Honestly…you're making a mess."

I sighed and walked over to the table, sitting down.

The thought of getting back into the car with Mum and Johnny, heading off to Harlech together like we were a family, made my heart sink. It didn't matter how much of an effort I made with Johnny, I was always going to feel like the little-kid-in-the-back, the add-on. Maybe I would be brave and go to the beach party. I seriously needed to find some friends while I was here.

"So finish your breakfast and get yourself ready, will you?" Mum said. "We're planning to head off in about twenty minutes." And she left the room.

I pulled my phone out of my pyjama pocket as soon as she went and I messaged Mia:

Help! I'm in Wales and it's dead and there is literally nothing to do... ☹

I waited a few minutes to see if she'd message me straight back and when she didn't I got up from the table and walked over to the sink, still eating my cereal. I looked out of the window. Johnny was sitting in the garden with his book. I watched him for a bit. It was so hard to understand how Mum and I had got to be on holiday with this man, who was basically a total stranger to me until six months ago. Dad dying had changed everything in so many ways. It had changed everything in an instant. One moment I was at school, it was a normal day, and then suddenly, it wasn't.

The memory of that day was etched in my head...I was in Art, and the Head came in. Everyone stopped what they were doing, looked up. I remember it was suddenly so quiet. And then she came over to me and spoke very gently and said I had to leave school. I had to go and meet my mum in the office. My dad was in hospital. And I nodded and I scooped up everything in front of me, everything from the desk, and I put it back into my pencil case, and I walked out, and then, well, time sort of distorted from there in my memory, because as soon as I knew he'd been knocked off his bike, hit by a car, everything changed. It never went back.

And it felt like things were still changing now. What had started off as Mum casually telling me she was just going for a drink with a friend from work, had now become this thing with Johnny where he was properly in our lives – coming round in the evening, at weekends, and now on this holiday – he was part of everything Mum and I did. Nothing was how I wanted it to be.

"I think I'll just look around on my own, if that's okay?" I said to Mum as we got out of the car in Harlech. I could see a couple of shops up ahead. It didn't look like there was a whole lot going on here, but I wanted to be on my own.

"Really? Well, okay," Mum said. "If you're sure."

"Yeah," I said. "I'm sure."

"If you want to come and meet us for a coffee or something then just text. I don't know how long we'll be, but I've got my phone," Mum said, and I watched her link arms with Johnny and walk off towards the castle. Johnny had been going on in the car about how much he wanted to go there.

I turned and headed in the other direction, and it became clear within about eight seconds that there wasn't really anything to do in Harlech, unless of course, like Johnny, a huge crumbling castle hanging on to a crag was your thing. Everything in the town seemed to be about the castle. Every sign seemed to be directing you back that way.

I carried on walking along the high street towards what looked like a little run of shops. It was high up here – I mean, I knew that from the steep lane we'd driven up to get into town, but now I was walking around I could see it, feel it, almost taste it in the cooler air of the wind. It was fresh. Different. And I had to admit that I kind of liked how you could see down to the wide beach through the gaps between the jumble of houses and shops – a view that put a blink of colour between the greys; chunks of white cloud hanging over a dark blue sea, and pale yellow dunes rolling along the coastline like a frame. It was almost a surprise each time it appeared to me in broken flashes between the buildings. And I guess I noticed it more because it wasn't like the shops were grabbing my attention. A half-filled supermarket, a newsagent full of plastic tubs holding fishing nets and buckets and spades and bats and balls. Seaside stuff, even though the sea wasn't that close when you were all the way up here. There was a junk shop too, with broken toys and tons of old-fashioned wine glasses, dirty and heavy, all sizes, and then some mad, random stuff – like pieces of armour, or a helmet of some kind. Lots of it just seemed like stuff that had got left behind. But in the front of the window were three bright green felt dragons wearing little red waistcoats holding signs that said *Welcome to Wales*. They cheered things up a bit. I had money to spend on this holiday, but I really didn't think I was going to be spending it here.

I carried on walking down the high street and back towards the castle now. The shops seemed to be thinning out a bit, but I decided to keep going, hoping for a cafe... And then something caught my eye – a photograph on a poster pinned to a noticeboard outside a shop.

Have you seen this girl?

I stepped forward to read...

A 17-year-old girl is missing from Barmouth...medium-length light brown hair, brown eyes, wearing blue jeggings, a pale blue T-shirt and trainers…thought to be carrying a shoulder bag made out of recycled jeans…

I looked at the photograph. There was something about the girl's face that looked kind of sad. No, not *kind of* sad, *really* sad. But I wondered if maybe I just saw that in her because she was missing. I read on – the girl had left home on Tuesday 5th August to go shopping, and hadn't returned since. It said someone matching her description had been spotted talking to a man in a blue car on the A496 heading towards Porthmadog just yesterday, but reports weren't yet confirmed and they were asking for more witnesses from the area… I didn't know where any of these places were, but I guessed they had to be near here.

I looked around. Suddenly I had no sense of how long I'd been standing in front of the poster. There were literally about three people passing by in the street, and no one seemed to have noticed me at all. *How strange,* I thought, *that in this quiet, out-of-the-way place, where it feels like nothing ever happens to anyone, this awful thing has happened.* It sounded like this girl had been taken. Did someone have her, and if they did, where had they gone?

I walked back along the street, and saw a smiling face coming towards me – Marko, I was pretty sure it was him – the boy from the cottage next door. He was wearing the same crazy bright clothes he'd been wearing when I'd seen him the day before.

"Hello again," he said. "So how are you liking Harlech?"

"It's seriously got it all going on here, right?" I said, smiling back.

Marko laughed. "You should go to the deli on the corner." He pointed down the street in the direction I was heading. "They do good ice cream. I'd show you, but I'm late. Just grabbing my lunch before I start my shift."

"It's fine," I said. "I'm sure I can find it. This place isn't exactly big."

"Right," Marko said, looking at me, still smiling, and then he didn't say anything else, and he didn't move, and we just stood there awkwardly kind of smiling at each other for no reason at all.

"So..." I said. "Your shift?"

I really wanted to break the awkward endlessly smiling moment.

"Yeah, I'm a lifeguard on Harlech Beach. Summer job." He pulled his phone out of his pocket and looked at it. "I start in about twenty minutes. Need a sandwich and to get down there now really, or I'm going to be late."

"So that explains the clothes," I said. "I didn't see that yesterday," and I pointed to his RNLI badge.

"Oh right, yeah," Marko said. "You didn't actually think I dressed like this out of choice, did you?"

I laughed. "No, no—"

"Oh, you did!" he said. "Nice!" And he laughed.

"No, I—"

I felt bad now, like I'd offended him, and he seemed really nice.

"So look, I've got to go, but you're coming to the party tonight, aren't you?" he said.

"Yes, well, maybe," I said, because I didn't know what else to say. It was definitely kind of tempting to think I might actually leave Mum and Johnny at the cottage tonight and go out. But then I wasn't going to know anyone at the party, apart from Marko, and it wasn't like I really knew him either. When I thought about it like that I was pretty sure I couldn't go. It was mad to think I'd turn up to a party on a beach that was literally full of strangers.

"I'll come and find you, then!" he said. "Later!"

And I found myself nodding and actually waving this time as he walked away. What the hell was I doing? I seriously needed Mia here so she could talk to me – tell me what to do.

I pulled out my phone. There was nothing back from her yet – no message. I scrolled through Snapchat; it was full of everyone else's pool pictures and blue skies in places way hotter than this, and I quickly came offline. I didn't want to see how much fun everyone else was having.

I looked up at the street. Seriously, if Mia could see where I was now… God, I missed her and Jade and all my friends. I missed London too. And this was only my first proper day here.

I took a deep breath, and told myself to stop my worst-case scenario thinking about Marko and the party and this place. I'd make a decision later about what I was going to do tonight. What I wanted now was an ice cream.

The deli Marko had mentioned was a two-minute walk from where we'd left each other. It didn't look like much from the outside, but as soon as I walked through the door I decided I was going to like it. There was a cabinet full of sandwiches, giant ones – great hunks of bread, fillings oozing out against their wrappers – and cakes on the counter covered in cream, and straight ahead a freezer lined with tubs of various brightly coloured ice creams. I could almost pretend I was in Ibiza with Mia when I looked at them. There were three small tables in the middle of the shop, an old couple sitting at one of them. They had their coats on while they nursed a large pot of tea. It was pretty dead in here, but the gorgeousness of the ice cream was making up for it.

"Hi. What can I get you?"

I looked up and saw a girl who seemed to have appeared from nowhere. She was standing behind the ice cream counter in a navy-blue apron, her hair tied back off her face.

"Excuse me, is our cake coming now?" one of the oldies called out to her.

"Oh, yes. Sorry. It's right here," she said, raising her eyebrows and smiling at me, as she headed over to them with two plates, each of them filled with a huge slab of cake. "Here you go."

I loved the sound of her voice. She was Welsh, but her accent was nothing like all that garbled shouting I'd heard yesterday when I'd switched on the TV. It was soft. Melodious even. And as she walked back round to the counter she looked at me again. "Sorry about that. What would you like?" she said, and I swear her eyes were sparkling, shining at me – emerald green and as bright as a bottle smashed against the rocks.

"I'll have the strawberries and cream," I said. "Double scoop, in a cone." As I said it I couldn't stop looking at her. She was just so pretty.

She handed the ice cream over and I gave her some cash.

"You can sit by the window, if you want," she said, and as she turned her back on me to get me my change, I thought about how much I'd like to look like her. Just like her.

I went over to the table by the window and got out my phone while I made a start on my ice cream. There was nothing from Mum, but there was a message now from Mia:

WTF?! Wales? What the hell are you doing there?

I messaged back quickly, hoping I'd catch her online.

Last-minute thing. Mum arranged it.
With Johnny... Cosy. Not.

I waited. Then I texted again.

I've been invited to a party. A beach party!

Jeez. They have those in Wales? Who invited you?

Some random called Marko.

Shit. Things move fast in Wales. How long you
been there...?

Got here yesterday... So do I go?

What's he like?

Seems nice.

Go.

I'm scared. I know NO ONE.

Come here! The parties are so good... ☺

I didn't text straight back. I wished I was in Ibiza. Another message came in from Mia.

Gotta go. Heading to the market. Tell me what happens!

And that was it. Mia was gone.

I looked up as the door of the deli opened with a clatter. A mum and her daughter came in and went up to the ice-cream counter. I watched. The daughter was probably only about six, holding her mum's hand while she chose her ice cream, her face pressed up against the glass. The pretty girl behind the counter chatted to them about their holiday, the weather, the beach, and I couldn't help but listen, glancing up every so often to look again while I started to flick through the pictures on my phone... They were from the end of term – Mia and Jade with Arjun and Louis in the park on the last day, our shirts covered in handwritten messages, stuffing ourselves with a whole load of popcorn and crisps. I smiled, remembering that day. It was weird to think that school was over now and that when we went back, we'd be going into different sixth-form colleges. Still together, but kind of apart.

"Everything okay?"

I looked up to see that the pretty girl was talking to me.

"Yeah," I said. "Thanks." I smiled back at her, getting up to leave, putting my phone in my bag. She was so different to all my friends back home. She was probably the same age as me, and yet everything about her was so completely different. I think it was her clothes, her hair. She was her own person. She was sure of herself and who she wanted to be.

I stepped out of the deli and the first thing I noticed was the wind. It had picked up. And it was cold. It felt like everything was being whipped by it and I guess I really noticed it because there was paper, lots of it, flapping about, off lamp posts, telegraph poles and shop windows. It was the same all the way up the street.

I walked back towards where Mum had parked the car. I pulled my hoody closer around me, the sound of the paper whipping about everywhere kind of freaking me out. I was sure it hadn't all been pinned to the shops and lamp posts when I'd walked this way before. Did the wind blowing like this mean there was a storm coming? It felt like it.

As I passed the next lamp post, I saw a poster for the missing girl, slightly different to the one I'd seen before. I looked ahead to the next lamp post. There was another. *Have you seen this girl?* I looked further up the street…all this paper, whipping around in the wind, it was all the same – posters with the photograph, the missing girl's face staring back at me from all over the street, and this time with her name, in big bold type – Ceri Rees.

I looked around. I wanted to see who was putting up the posters… I guessed it must have been her family, her friends, or maybe even volunteers, desperately hoping to find her. I wondered if I'd just missed seeing them when I'd walked up the high street before. Or whether they had all been put up while I was in the deli looking at my phone, eating my ice cream.

I said her name in my head.

Ceri Rees.

She was missing now, but they could find her – her friends, her family. It was awful that she'd gone missing, but there was hope. It wasn't the same for me. Dad was gone. Forever gone. And as I walked to the car I wished for Ceri and her family that they would find each other soon. If I couldn't have that, then I wanted it for Ceri and her family. I wanted it for all of them.

3

Marko knocked for me at around 5 p.m. to see if I was coming to the party. He said he'd come back at 7 p.m. so we could head to the beach together, which was good, because I didn't know the way from the cottage. But it felt like we were going on a date, which was weird for so many reasons, but mainly because, well, clearly this wasn't a date. And on top of that I didn't know what to wear to a beach party, and that was stressing me out too.

In my head, a beach party meant shorts and little bikini tops and flip-flops, and probably some kind of outfit that I'd never be seen dead in, but of course that was a beach party in my head, Ibiza style. I was pretty sure the most important thing I was going to want to take to a beach party in North Wales was going to be my hoody and my phone. So I grabbed both of those and pulled on my jeans and a T-shirt that Mia told me really brought out the colour of my eyes – it was a kind of pale almost washed out blue – and it had this big silver star on the front.

I pulled out my phone.

I'm going to the party. Wearing the silver-star top. Wish me luck. Scared. Wish I was in Ibiza with you. xx

"So, you ready?" Marko said when I answered the door at seven.

"Yeah," I said, and I smiled, but I think it came out more like some kind of weird grimace. I couldn't tell. It was nerves more than anything else.

"Let's go," he said.

I called out to Mum, to let her know I was heading off.

"Hang on!" she said, and she suddenly appeared in the hall from the kitchen.

"Hello," she said, looking at Marko now. "I'm Tasha, Cait's Mum."

Marko nodded and reached out his hand to shake Mum's, and I felt like I was in a scene from some American high-school movie. Like I was getting picked up for prom, except I wasn't in a crazy over-the-top meringue of a dress, thank god, and Marko wasn't all tidied up in a suit.

"Nice to meet you," Marko said. "I'm Marko – staying next door."

"Great," Mum said. "So are you here on holiday too? When did you arrive?"

Mum was giving him the third degree.

"Oh, got here in July, and I'm not leaving until the end of August. I'm a lifeguard, on Harlech Beach. My dad lives here," he said, "but I come and stay in the holidays – I've been coming for years. I used to just hang out, but now I'm here to work *and* hang out. Lifeguarding is a good summer job to have."

"Sounds it," Mum said.

"So I'm at the beach a lot of the time, and Dad's a bit of a recluse in the summer as he writes, but if you need to know anything about the area, and you see one of us, then just ask," he said and he smiled.

"Well, it's nice to meet you," Mum said. "Now, you're going to be down on the beach, right? What time do you think it'll finish? You won't be too late, will you?"

This was all getting so much worse.

"It's on the beach, yeah," Marko said. "Not the main beach at Harlech. It's in the cove, closer to here, just on the other side of the headland where the estuary goes out."

He pointed to where the land jutted out on the horizon. "We'll walk across the fields. It's quicker than walking along the road from here."

Mum nodded.

"Okay," she said, but I could tell she wasn't that happy.

There was a pause. I shifted slightly on my feet, waiting for her to release us from the questioning.

"I'll go and wait for you over by the gate," Marko said, looking at me, and he wandered off, nodding a goodbye back to Mum. "Come over when you're ready, Cait."

"Sure," I said. It was actually a massive relief that he'd stepped away. I really didn't want him to witness any more of Mum's extreme fussing. She'd got worse since Dad had died, and even though I could understand why, it still didn't seem to make it any less embarrassing in front of other people.

"I think you should text me when you're ready to come home," Mum said. "Johnny has offered to pick you up, which is nice of him, isn't it?"

"Right," I said.

I wasn't going to start praising Johnny for offering to pick me up. No way. I just wanted to get out of there.

"But not too late, Cait. I'd like you back before twelve. Actually, look – take this," and she stuffed her hand into the back pocket of her jeans and handed me a twenty-pound note. "Take it so you've got some cash for a taxi. Just in case."

"Thanks," I said. "Look...Marko's waiting. I think I better go..."

"Yes, sure," she said. "Have fun."

I nodded and walked towards Marko, stuffing the twenty-pound note into my bag. I was glad I had the money for a taxi now. There was absolutely no way I was going to let Johnny pick me up later.

"You ready?" Marko said, smiling.

"Yeah," I said. "She's a bit of a worrier, you know? Really sorry about that."

"It's fine. They're all like that, aren't they?"

"Yeah, I guess so." I was glad that Marko seemed pretty chilled about the way Mum had been. But then, as we walked into the field, I heard a *clink clink clink* – the chime of bottle against bottle in his rucksack – and realized that Mum behaving as she had wasn't the only embarrassing thing that had happened so far this evening.

"I didn't bring anything to drink," I said. "I mean, I forgot. I don't suppose there's a shop anywhere... somewhere...on the way?" I screwed up my face. We were in a field. Clearly there were no shops anywhere.

"Don't worry," he said. "You can have some of mine. I'm sure there'll be plenty to share around to be honest.

And no – no shops in these fields, I'm afraid…" he said, laughing, pulling a cheeky sort of a face.

"Right, stupid thing to say," I said.

God, it was just about the stupidest stupid thing to say. We carried on walking.

"So if we cut across these fields there's a gate in the bottom one and we can drop down to the cove from there," Marko said.

"Great," I said. "I'd never have found the way on my own."

"It's finding your way back that's more of a challenge. It gets pretty dark here at night, but if it's clear the sky will look amazing on the way home."

"I've got money for a taxi…and…" I hesitated because I didn't want to mention Johnny and the possibility of getting picked up. And also the thought of how dark it would be walking back later freaked me out, aside from the fact that at this point I still hardly knew Marko at all.

"So do you get taxis everywhere in London, then?" Marko said.

"No!" I said, laughing. I wasn't sure if he was winding me up or not. "Night buses. No shops in fields and no such thing as night buses around here, I guess?"

"You're lucky to get a bus in daylight here," Marko said.

"But of course at night you do get the stars," and he was smiling. "They really do light the way."

I looked up at him and smiled back. And for a moment I thought that maybe seeing the stars with him wouldn't be so bad.

"So, you see those boats, over on the other side of the estuary?" he said, pointing towards the water as we came over the top of the first field. "That's Porthmadog. They rebuilt the toll bridge across the estuary a few years ago. You can get from this side straight into Snowdonia. Used to cost five pence. Costs nothing now."

I nodded. Marko obviously really liked it here. It was kind of cute the way he was showing me things, telling me about the place.

"Did you see all those posters in town today, about the missing girl?" I said. "They said that she was last seen talking to a man in a car going towards Porthmadog. I had wondered if it was close by."

Marko shook his head. "The missing girl?"

"Yeah. Didn't you see the posters in Harlech today?"

Marko kind of shrugged. "No, I didn't notice them. But I guess I was rushing to get my lunch, get to my shift, and then I saw you and I got, well, I got distracted..." and he looked at me and it felt kind of awkward and I wasn't sure whether he was actually paying me a compliment or not. I mean, I liked the way he seemed to be saying I had grabbed all of his attention, but was that really what he was saying? I wasn't sure.

"I'm surprised," I said, "that you didn't see the posters. They were everywhere by the time I left town, blowing around in the wind." I stepped off the stile we'd just both climbed over to get into the next field and looked up at him.

"Strange," he said, looking straight back at me. "I didn't notice any posters. I didn't see a thing."

The cove was a tiny horseshoe of a beach tucked into craggy grey rocks. As soon as we got to the edge of the final field and clambered down the sloping slates on to the sand, Marko started to walk a little faster, ahead of me, looking around. There must have been about twenty or so people there. I guessed he was looking for someone he knew, and I suddenly felt like a complete oddball, a stranger, and I wished I hadn't come. It was intimidating seeing all these people I didn't know, standing or sitting in groups, their bags dumped down around them, surrounded by food and drink, chatting, building fires for a barbecue, playing music.

"Come on, let's head over this way," Marko said suddenly, and he started to stride towards two people who'd got a fire going a little away from everyone else, on the far side of the cove.

"Hey!" Marko called out as we got closer. I followed

and smiled at a boy, and then a girl, who both looked up at the sound of Marko's voice, and jumped to their feet to greet him, the girl throwing her arms around his neck.

"Alright?" she said, giving him a quick kiss on the cheek, before stepping back. It was then that I recognized her – the girl from the deli; the ridiculously pretty girl I hadn't been able to stop looking at, who'd served me my ice cream.

"Alright, Marko," said the boy, shaking Marko's hand in this really formal way and then sitting back down on the sand by the fire.

I wondered if Marko was going to introduce me, but he didn't, and as he sat down on the sand I decided to just sit down next to him. The boy looked up at me, expectantly.

"Hi," I said. "I'm Cait."

"Ifan," he said, and I nodded, and I looked up at the girl, who was still standing in the space where she and Marko had been hugging just a moment ago. She paused for a minute, looking at me, and then came and sat down next to Ifan.

"I'm Hannah," she said and she gave me a quick smile that wasn't really a smile at all.

"Hannah works in the deli," Marko said. "Where they sell the amazing ice cream. Did you go, by the way?"

"Yeah, I did. I saw you today actually…" I said, now

looking at Hannah. "You served me, you probably don't remember—"

"Today?" Hannah said, and she looked directly at me again. "No, sorry. I don't remember you." She smiled at Marko, and then laughed. "I mean, I'm not being rude or anything, but I don't remember you at all." And somehow in the way she said it, she sounded really rude. I wondered for a moment how she'd done that. Said one thing, but totally implied another.

"So…" Hannah said, looking at Marko now, and then looking at me, "Cait is…?"

"Sorry – yeah," Marko said. "Cait is staying in the cottage next to Dad's. She arrived yesterday."

"You on holiday?" Ifan said.

I nodded. Ifan and Hannah had pretty strong Welsh accents. It made me realize that Marko didn't have an accent at all. I hadn't really noticed that until now.

"Where you from? London by any chance?" Ifan said.

"Yup, London," I said.

"I love London," Hannah said. "I've only been once, mind you."

"It's where I've always lived, so I guess I'm lucky, really," I said.

Hannah nodded. "You are. I'd like to live there. So much going on. Not like here."

I wondered where Marko was from. I hadn't asked him before.

Ifan looked up. "You think you'd like it busy all the time, Hannah, but I reckon you wouldn't. All those cars, all those people. I reckon you like the idea of London more than the reality."

"Yeah, maybe. I didn't like the tube much," Hannah said. "It stunk."

"Not many people like the tube," I said. "Even Londoners." Hannah smiled and it felt like in some small way I might have slightly won her over, and it pleased me, because I really felt like I needed to win her over somehow.

"So are there lots of people here you all know?" I asked, glancing around us at everyone gathered in their groups in the cove.

"Some from sixth form," Ifan said. "But we don't hang around with them all that much. It's hard not to all end up in the same place when word of a beach party gets out. You know, small place, small school, and all that."

I knew what Ifan meant. Mia and Jade and I were a three, we were solid, friends since Year Seven, but we were looking forward to breaking away from everyone else and going to a new sixth form, meeting some new people next year. Easier to do that in a bigger place like

London. But I didn't say anything and there was silence, and suddenly it felt kind of awkward.

"Which is why it's nice that we've met you, Cait," Marko said, filling the silence, and I nodded, embarrassed that he was making me the centre of attention, and because Ifan and Hannah were both looking at me. "Someone new to hang out with," he said.

"Yeah," I said, and I smiled.

"Like Alys," Ifan said, and I looked over at him as he said it and saw Hannah and Marko share a look between them.

"Alys?" I said.

It felt like the whole atmosphere had suddenly changed.

Ifan took a swig of his beer, and then jammed the bottle in the sand between his feet, looking down.

"So who's Alys?" I asked, because seriously, no one had replied.

"Just some girl we met last summer," Hannah said. "She hung out with us for a bit."

I nodded and looked at Marko, but he was looking across at Hannah now, like he was trying to reassure her or something.

Ifan was swirling his beer bottle around, making circles on circles in the sand.

"Kind of like you're doing now," Ifan said, looking up

for a moment. "Joining our gang. Except Alys was different."

"Different how?" I said.

Ifan didn't reply. It felt awkward again. But I didn't know what he meant. Did he mean that she was different-good? And I was different-bad? It felt that way. It felt like Ifan had given me a little jab, a little punch to the stomach. It didn't seem to matter that Marko had invited me here – in about three minutes flat Hannah had been kind of rude and Ifan had made me feel like a complete hanger-on.

"So, is she coming tonight?" I asked, for something to say rather than anything else. And because I wondered whether maybe I'd like Alys more than I liked Ifan and Hannah right now. Maybe Alys would be more my sort of person. More like me.

"No," Hannah said. "Or at least, not as far as we know, but we really don't know that much."

'Right," I said, not really understanding why this all seemed to be so torturous.

"She left kind of suddenly," Ifan said, carrying on playing with his bottle in the sand. "Last summer."

"So what happened?" I said, because clearly there was something going on, but no one was really saying what it was, and I really wanted to know now.

"Just forget it," Hannah said. "Ifan should never have mentioned it."

I looked at Marko. Why did it seem like I'd completely put my foot in it just by asking?

"So, listen, who needs a drink?" he said, grabbing the bag he'd brought from behind him. "I've got beers and a bottle of wine from my dad's stash too." He pulled a cheeky kind of face and it made me smile and completely changed the mood.

"I'll have a beer," I said. "If that's okay."

"Sure," Marko said. He threw a bottle over to me and I caught it, and the bottle opener too, and he laughed and suddenly I didn't care how spiky Hannah was, or how unfriendly Ifan seemed to be. I liked Marko, and I was glad to be here at the party with him rather than back at the cottage with Mum and Johnny. I wondered for a moment whether he might feel the same way too.

"So shall we start to walk back?" Marko asked.

The fire had died down, and Hannah had gone off. I'd watched her throughout the evening, flitting between groups like a social fairy, throwing her head back, playing with her hair, enjoying all the obvious attention. She was so pretty but somehow, now that I'd talked to her, she seemed less pretty than before. And Ifan seemed more relaxed without her. Or maybe it was just that he'd had a few beers. It was hard to tell.

"Shall we go?" Marko said again.

I looked up. I hadn't decided yet whether I'd walk with Marko or get a taxi. I hadn't dared look at my phone all night because I didn't want to know what time it was, or if Mum had texted. It was dark now. It had been for a bit. I guessed it must have been coming up for 10 p.m., maybe even 11 p.m. It can't have been midnight yet.

Ifan stood up. "I'm gonna head off," he said.

"Night." And he left, fast.

"Is he okay?" I said, looking at Marko. "He seems kind of, I don't know, quiet…"

"Yeah, he's fine," Marko said. "That's just Ifan. You should get to know him while you're here. He's really nice."

I felt bad. It was stupid of me to have made a comment about Ifan, who I hardly knew, to Marko, who I hardly knew either. I shivered slightly.

"You cold?"

I nodded. Despite what was left of the fire, my hands and my face were freezing cold now, although I did feel kind of warm inside, from the beer.

"A walk over the fields is always just what I need at this point in the night," Marko said, standing up. "It warms you up and of course the stars are amazing out here."

"You seriously love the stars!" I said, interrupting and laughing, not moving off the sand.

"Are you taking the piss?" he said, smiling.

"No, no," I said. "But that is like the fifth time you've mentioned them!"

"Okay," he said, and he stretched his hand out to pull me up. "You're right. It's because of my mum. She always talked about how different they were back home."

I took Marko's hand and let him pull me up quickly,

letting go once I was standing. "Back home, where?"

"Croatia. My parents are from there – from before, when it was Yugoslavia. I was born in the UK, but Croatia's home for them. Listen, shall we walk or do you want to call for that taxi? You can usually get a signal once you get onto the main road. I can walk with you up the lane to the road from here."

"I don't know," I said, pulling at my bag, finding my phone, and then seeing I had no messages, because I had no signal, just as Marko had said. It was gone 11.30 p.m. I looked up. "I'm not really sure what to…"

"To be honest, by the time we've walked to the road to get a signal and called a cab we could be halfway back to the cottages. I'll totally wait with you for a cab, but it would be quicker to walk, if it's time you're worried about?"

I wasn't worried about the time. I just wasn't sure about walking back across the fields with Marko in the pitch black. I'd had a great evening, but I still didn't know him that well, and I was kind of out of my comfort zone in this much wide open space, in this much dark. But then the thought of maybe not being able to get a cab straight away, and the possibility of Mum sending Johnny out to pick me up like some kind of search party freaked me out more.

"Let's walk," I said. "And you can tell me about your mum and about Croatia and what it's like. I've never been."

We walked across the sand towards the gate in the bottom field.

"My mum and dad came here in 1991. They were in their twenties."

"And they came to Wales?" I asked.

"No, Birmingham. My dad had just started to lecture at Split University when the unrest began. It was only because of his connections within the university, and the links it had with the UK, that he could find a way out of the country quickly, and with my mum too. They were lucky. Others weren't so lucky."

"I really don't know that much about it all, I mean, what happened..." I said. "During the war—?"

I felt like I should have known more.

"Genocides," Marko said. "Mass murders, mass graves. Atrocities – that's what they call them on the news. That's what they were."

I nodded.

I didn't say anything because I didn't know what to say.

We walked together in silence for a moment, the only sound between us made by the grasses in the field brushing rhythmically against our legs.

"I'm sorry," I said, looking up.

"Yeah, me too," Marko said. "But you know, mainly for my mum." He paused. "It's kind of weird, because my mum and my dad lost so much family, and their family is *my* family too, but I was never there and I never knew them, and so I don't feel the same."

I nodded.

"But my mum will never forget," he said. "Cousins, aunts, brothers, friends, all lost. We came to Birmingham and we've stayed there. That's where mum and I still live now. She says she never wants to go back to Croatia, that she can't, but that leaves her forever stuck here, thinking about the past, wishing for a future she knows she can never have. I think that's why she's always looking up at the sky. Somehow in the stars there's some kind of connection to the country that she loves, the places that feel like home to her, the places where she belongs – it's all up there for her. It's like it holds all the memories of the people that she's loved and lost..." Marko looked at me and shrugged. "I don't know if I'm making any sense. It's kind of hard to explain."

"You are," I said. "And what about your dad?"

"He sees it differently. He's lost people too, of course, but he's always looked forward not back. They're not together any more. I'm not sure if it's what broke them up – their differences about home, and what happened. I've never asked. But when they separated Dad moved here, to Wales. He used to lecture, but he mostly writes now. He likes it here. He likes the isolation. And of course I visit in the holidays. I come most summers, usually Easter too. I've been coming for years."

"And that's how you know Hannah and Ifan?"

"I got chatting to Ifan at this cafe on Harlech Beach, the Coffee Shack. You'll definitely get to go while you're here. Ifan works there now, and before he worked there he used to just hang out there – a lot. I did too. We got talking, and then he introduced me to Hannah."

"You all seem to know each other really well," I said.

"Yeah, we do," Marko said, and I looked across and I saw him smile, and I thought about how, when we'd arrived at the beach, Hannah had jumped up to greet him, thrown her arms around his neck, kissed him.

Marko went on. "You know, I think Dad moved here because this place had good memories for him. We used to come to Porthmadog on holiday when I was younger, as a family. We were really happy here."

I nodded, thinking about London, about home. Our house in London held all my memories, all the good ones with Dad. I liked remembering that it was there, waiting for us – for me and Mum – when we got back, despite Johnny being around.

"I'm lucky," Marko said. "I have two places I can call home – Birmingham and here."

We carried on walking in silence for a bit. The air was cool, but it felt nice now that we were walking. Fresh. I thought about the missing girl – her face on the poster today. I wondered where she was right now, if she was okay.

"You've gone quiet," Marko said, and he looked over at me.

I looked up. "I was just thinking about the girl who's gone missing," I said. "I've thought about her a few times since I saw those posters earlier today."

Marko nodded. "You know there are people going missing all the time, hundreds and hundreds of them, every day, everywhere, people experiencing the most terrible things. Just look at the news – Syria, Afghanistan, the Rohingya crisis—"

"I know," I said. "But every person has someone who cares about them, misses them, grieves for them. It doesn't matter whether it's one person in Wales or hundreds of people somewhere else in the world. Every person counts, right?"

"Right," Marko said, and he smiled. "Sorry – I think what I just said is the kind of thing my mum would say. She's always thinking about Croatia, the bigger picture."

I nodded.

Marko went on. "I don't feel the same as my mum, but it doesn't mean I've forgotten what happened to all those people there. For one, my mum will never let me forget."

"And it's right not to forget," I said, looking up at Marko now. "Even if you've lost just one person, you should never forget."

Marko nodded, and as we walked I could feel him just that bit closer to me, almost nudging me, his arm gently bumping against mine as we walked. We were nearly back at the cottages now, but in those final few moments, just walking with Marko, in a quiet kind of silence, felt nice.

"So," Marko said as we climbed over the gate and onto the gravel in front of the cottages. "How about coming down to Harlech Beach tomorrow? I'm working, but the weather's meant to be good – less wind, more calm. I've got a wetsuit in the lifeguard hut you can borrow if you want to swim. The water is pretty cold. I could buy you a drink at the Coffee Shack after?"

"Sounds good," I said, and as I went to leave I felt Marko's hand softly wrap itself around mine and squeeze it.

"Night," he said, and I smiled and squeezed his hand back. "See you tomorrow then."

"Yeah," I said, letting go of his hand. And as I walked towards the front door of the cottage, for some reason I found myself smiling…smiling and smiling.

"Is that you, Cait?"

Mum's voice was calling out to me as soon as I got into the hall.

"Yup!" I shouted back.

"I was just about to send out a search party!"

I went into the sitting room.

"By which I mean Johnny," Mum said laughing, turning round to look at me, and stroking Johnny's face gently as she did. I could see she'd had a few glasses of wine. She was curled up on the sofa with him, her head on his chest, their legs entwined, as they lay together watching TV.

My smile went.

"I'm going to get some water and go up to bed," I said, quickly walking towards the door. I hated seeing Mum and Johnny like this. I wanted to get out of the room.

"Night, lovely," Mum called back, and then I heard her immediately turn to Johnny and say something about what they were watching on TV and laugh, and him laughing with her.

"Close the door, will you, Cait?" Johnny said. "There's a terrible draught."

I closed the door and went straight up to my room, slipping off my shoes, and I climbed into bed and under the duvet in all my clothes. The house was cold, and I couldn't be bothered to get undressed. I wanted Dad. I wanted him so much it actually hurt, like someone or something was pushing down hard on me, on my chest. And I hated Johnny. I hated him so much. I hated him for being here and I hated him for acting like he could fill the Dad-shaped hole in our lives, because he couldn't. He wouldn't. No one ever could.

I took a deep breath in, and looked at my phone. There was a message from Mia.

How was the beach party?

I typed…

It was good. But then I got back and Mum and Johnny kind of killed the mood…

And then I backspaced and deleted it all, putting my phone on the side. I'd reply in the morning when my head felt clearer, because right now all I could think about was Dad. It was still so hard to believe that he wouldn't ever be coming back. That he wouldn't just turn up one day, walk in through the door, ask me how it was all going, wind me up, make me laugh, like he'd never actually gone...

I thought about Marko and his mum and his family. All those people – lost – in one way or another. And then I thought about Ceri Rees, and I wished for Ceri's family that there would be some kind of happy ending. Because I really wanted to believe in happy endings. I wanted to believe in those more than anything else at all.

SUNDAY

6

Harlech Beach was huge – I mean I knew it was from the view up in town – but when I walked over the dunes and saw the expanse of sand before me, filled with windbreaks, dogs, people…I felt lost. I looked to the left, trying to search out a couple of small sheds or Portakabins set back from the water – the lifeguard hut and the cafe. I was pretty sure they'd be somewhere along the main stretch of the beach close to where I was standing…

"Hey!"

I heard a voice and immediately recognized it as a massively amplified and slightly robotic version of Marko's. It was coming from my right. I turned towards it, and saw Marko, back in his bright clothes, with a megaphone in his hand, waving wildly at me, the lifeguard hut behind him, and another bigger shed, set a little further back, with a sign on the front of it – *The Coffee Shack*. I walked over to him.

"So, you found us. Sorry, I didn't exactly explain where the hut was last night, did I?" Marko said and he was smiling at me. A warm, wide smile.

"No, but it's fine," I said. "Even if you had explained I'm sure I wouldn't have remembered."

"Bit pissed, were you?" a voice said from behind.

I looked up. It was Ifan. He'd stepped out of the hut, holding a black and orange wetsuit in his hands.

"No, not really," I said, looking quickly at Marko. I didn't want him to think that I hadn't remembered our walk home across the fields, our conversation, our goodbye. "Maybe just a bit fuzzy around the edges," I said. "But, you know, in a good way."

"Right," Ifan said, and he grinned at Marko, and I wondered what Marko had said to him about me, but actually when I thought about it again, I didn't care. It was better to be piggy in the middle here, like this, right now, with Marko and Ifan, than back at the cottage with Mum and Johnny, or sitting somewhere completely on my own. So I decided I'd take it – however it was going to be with these new people, with Ifan and Hannah – because Marko was nice and right now anything was better than being alone.

"So do you want to borrow a wetsuit?" Ifan said, looking at me now. "Marko said you might. The good thing about being a friend of Marko's is that you can hang out here and borrow all this stuff for free."

I smiled. "Yeah," I said. "That would be great."

"I just got this one out for me, but I'm pretty sure there's another one in there somewhere. I'll just go and find it."

Ifan disappeared into the hut again, and Marko looked at me and I looked back at him and as we stood there together I went blank. I couldn't think of a single thing to say... I opened my mouth to talk, not sure what was going to come out, when suddenly there was a voice shouting from up the beach...

"Marko! Marko!"

I turned to see Hannah. She was running now, the sand stopping her from moving at the speed she was clearly aiming for; it slipped around and under her feet, slowing her down.

"Marko!"

Her voice was urgent. Marko started walking towards her.

"What is it? Is everything okay?" Marko said as they met a little way up from the hut. And then I watched Hannah put her hand on Marko's arm, pulling him with her towards the hut, almost dragging him along as she went.

"Is Ifan with you?" she said to Marko, ignoring me as they approached now. She had a piece of paper in her hand, her breath kind of short from the running.

"Yeah," Marko said. "He's getting Cait a wetsuit. What is it?"

Ifan stepped out of the hut. "Hi, Hannah," he said, and then he handed me a dark-purple wetsuit. "Here, try this."

I took the wetsuit from him and wondered how the hell I was going to get into it without entering a whole world of pain.

I looked up again to try and say something to Hannah, to say hi or something, but she was still ignoring me, so I decided I'd say nothing. I'd ignore her too.

I looked for the zip on the wetsuit, pretending like I wasn't there, like I wasn't bothered that Hannah was acting as if I didn't even exist.

"Have you seen this? Seriously?" Hannah said to Marko. "Have you seen it?" Her voice was high and urgent.

I glanced up to see what she was talking about, what she was showing Marko, pushing in his face. And as I looked I could see it was the poster of the missing girl – of Ceri Rees.

I looked quickly at Marko.

"That's the poster I was telling you about, Marko," I said. "The one I saw all over town yesterday."

I looked at Hannah.

"They're everywhere, aren't they?" Then I sort of kicked myself for talking. I was meant to be ignoring her. I'd completely failed.

Hannah stepped forward, closer to where Marko was standing next to Ifan, and she pushed the poster right up in both their faces.

"Seriously, look! Look at this picture and tell me what you see!"

Marko and Ifan just stood there, looking, saying nothing.

"Look!" Hannah said again.

"It's Ceri Rees," I said. "That's her name. Ceri Rees." I couldn't stop myself from butting in.

"Look at it, Marko!" Hannah said again. "Ifan, look at the picture! I swear to god, look at it! Can't you see? It's Alys! I swear to god it's Alys!"

PART
TWO

LAST
SUMMER

HANNAH

AT THE LAKE

She interrupted us. This girl. I'd never seen her before, and I couldn't believe she did that.

"Do you know if they sell cold drinks?"

She walked right up to us, to me, Marko and Ifan, walked right into the middle of our conversation, and asked us some idiotic question about whether the Coffee Shack did cold drinks or not. I mean, *what?* It's called the Coffee Shack, and yes, it does look like a shack, but it's not *only* going to sell coffee just because it's got the word "coffee" in its name, right?

"Yeah, there's plenty of cold drinks inside," Ifan said, because Ifan loved the Coffee Shack, and that wasn't just because he worked there and thought it was the best place in the world, it was because it gave him a place to hang out with people. Ifan wasn't exactly sociable. He was fine with me because we'd known each other since the beginning of time. And he got on with Marko, because

Marko was, well, Marko – basically he's lush and everyone loves him. I've never really worked out why Ifan is like he is – kind of shy. He just is.

"There's pop and loads of fruit juices," Ifan said, and he smiled at her – the girl – proving my theory that talking about what you could buy at the Coffee Shack was basically the best way into Ifan's world – should you want to go there.

I looked up at the girl again, expecting her to say thanks to Ifan, go inside, buy the cold drink, and go away. But she didn't move. She looked over at the Coffee Shack and then back at Ifan, like she was thinking about going in, but she wasn't ready to just yet. Like *what*? So I waited to carry on talking, finish what I was saying, and while I waited she just kept on standing there, like she was holding on for someone or something – except none of us knew what it was. She was seriously, well…weird. She was wearing these shabby-looking clothes – all blacks and greys. The only colour on her were these daps she was wearing with green laces; they must have been pale yellow or white originally, but now they were seriously minging – well beyond saving – and she'd drawn all over them; all these strange designs – all circles and curls, like some kind of manic doodle.

Ifan looked at me, and I pulled a face back at him,

like – *Can we carry on our conversation now?* Ifan knew how to read my faces. He knew me *that* well. Except now I couldn't even remember what we were talking about. I opened my mouth to talk anyway, but Ifan turned away from me suddenly and looked back up at the girl. I hated that he did that – ignored me.

"You okay?" he said. "Do you want me to come in with you? Show you where the drinks are? I work here, I mean, not today, I'm not working right now, but…I can show you."

"No," the girl said. "It's fine. I'll go in and get one and I'll be back in a minute," and she went inside.

"Who was that?" Marko said, looking at Ifan.

"No idea," Ifan said.

"You acted like you knew her," Marko said, and Ifan shook his head and looked round again towards the door of the Shack.

"She's not seriously going to come back and sit with us, is she?" I said, looking at Marko for backup.

Ifan shrugged. "Why not?"

I shared another look, this time with Marko, a look that said seriously *what the…*? And before he could say anything or give me the same look back, she was there again, and Marko was staring past me, and straight at her.

"Hey," he said.

And then the girl pulled up a chair from one of the other tables and joined us. What the hell?

"I'm Marko," Marko said now, smiling.

"Alright, I'm Alys," the girl said.

There was a silence.

"And you?" she said, looking at me.

"Hannah," I said. "And this is Ifan."

"Er, thanks, Hannah," Ifan said. "I think I can introduce myself." And he smiled at Alys.

"Oh, sorry, yeah – I was talking for him," I said quickly. "Old habit. We've known each other for *years*. We're like brother and sister, me and Ifan. Well, kind of. We're good friends. Really good friends." And I smiled.

Alys cracked open her can of pop and took a sip. She really didn't look like she was bothered about anything but herself.

"So do you live round here?" Marko said. "Or have you just come to the beach for the day?"

We'd all clocked the accent. In the summer our ears were well tuned to who was a visitor here and who was local.

Alys nodded, taking another sip from her can. "Yeah, I'm from down the coast – Barmouth."

"Nice beach there," Marko said.

"He's a lifeguard," I said. "Knows all the beaches around here."

Alys nodded again. "Yeah, it's nice at Barmouth," she said. "Busy though."

"And you thought it would be less busy here?" I said, and I laughed, looking at Marko and Ifan to laugh with me, because Harlech Beach was just as busy as Barmouth in the summer – *everyone* knew that. But it was like they weren't really with me on it. I stopped. "I guess everywhere is busy though, this time of year. That's what I meant, like." I looked again at Ifan and Marko to back me up, but they were giving me nothing.

"Yeah, but there's a lot more beach here at Harlech than at Barmouth," Ifan said. "So you know, it's busy, but there's more space for everyone to hang out." I watched him look at Alys and smile again and she smiled back at him and I wondered whether that was the most he'd ever said to someone he'd only just met inside, say, ten minutes, *ever*. I reckoned it was.

"So obviously I'm biased, but I think Harlech Beach has definitely got it all going on," Marko said, nodding in agreement with Ifan.

"Yeah. And it has the Coffee Shack, so it is absolutely the place to be," Ifan said, still smiling. Or was he grinning now? I swear he was grinning. And I looked over at

Marko and he was doing it too. Did they both fancy her? It felt like Marko was flirting; flirting like he had sometimes with me. But I couldn't really tell with Ifan, because I'd never seen him flirt before. The whole thing was making me feel a bit sick.

"I like it," Alys said, looking around her. "For a beach full of people, families, dogs and all that stuff…and the sand is pretty nice…I mean I'd rather be on an empty beach somewhere hot, like really hot, but yeah…" I looked over at Marko and Ifan and they were both looking at her, nodding, like stupid nodding dogs, like the ones my nan has on the back shelf of her car.

"Well I'd much rather be in Bali, but you know…" I said, trying to pull Ifan and Marko back to me. But it wasn't working.

"So what are you all doing? Just hanging out here for the day?" Alys said.

"Yeah, well, it's my day off, so—" Marko said, before Alys interrupted him.

"I was going to hang out at the beach today too," Alys said, "but now I'm thinking about it, I want to do something different." Alys looked at us. "Are any of you up for something different?"

Ifan was doing the nodding thing again.

"Do you know the lakes behind Harlech?" she said.

"It's like being in another world up there. There's no one else around. It's not like the beach. Up there it's just these beautifully still lakes and these huge mountains…all this space."

Ifan looked at Marko now. "I'm up for that," he said. "Definitely."

"I—" I went to speak, but Alys went on.

"There's one lake I know… We should go there. Let's go now… Has anyone got a car? We'd need to drive. Who here can drive?" Alys stood up, and her face kind of lit up.

"We've got plans, haven't we?" I said, leaning forward, looking at Marko, putting my hand on his arm to pull his attention over to me, to stop this virtual hell from happening, because I really didn't want to go into the mountains with this girl we didn't know.

"Have we?" Ifan said, looking over at me now. "I didn't think we had any plans. And I like Alys's plan. I'm up for it. I can borrow my mum's car. It's just up in town."

"Well, yeah, but maybe another day, don't you think, Marko?" I said, trying to hide the look that I knew was crawling all over my face, the *What the hell? Who is this girl? What do you mean go into the mountains?* look.

"I don't know," Marko said. "I mean, I'm free, we're all free today, aren't we?" He was looking from me to Ifan and I could see that he actually wanted to go.

"I haven't been up into the mountains for years. Not since I was a kid," Ifan said. "Marko, have you ever been?"

Marko shook his head.

"You'll love it," Ifan said.

"So let's do it," Alys said, and she picked up her can, taking a few large gulps then banging it down on the table.

Ifan stood up. "We'll just need to go back to my house, get the car."

"Sure," Alys said, and then she turned to look at Marko and me. "You coming?"

We were both still sitting down at the table.

Marko turned to me. "Come on, Hannah. It won't be any fun without you."

And somehow I found myself saying yes, even though I really didn't want to go at all.

Ifan brought the car down to the lower road to pick us all up. I got in the back with Marko. I would have got in the front, but Alys stepped up and got in there first. I watched her put her seat belt on, and look over at Ifan as she did. She definitely wanted Ifan to look at her, but he was messing about with the car. I think in that moment I saw a flash of something – I thought she looked helpless.

But I guess I'm not a hundred per cent sure.

"So I kind of know where I'm heading for, but you'll probably have to direct me once I'm out the other side of town," Ifan said, pulling back onto the road.

"Okay," Alys said, and she was looking out of the window like the world was pulling at her, pulling her gaze outwards. She was with us, but also somehow not.

"So did you come from Barmouth today, Alys?" I said, to try and make some kind of conversation.

Alys shook her head. "No. I'm staying in Llanbedr this week. Holiday."

Marko nodded.

"Whereabouts?" I asked.

"Caravan park. Just some crappy old statics in a field, but you know, it's fine."

Ifan smiled and looked over at Alys and I watched her drink his smile in and smile back, and I thought about how weird it was that Ifan liked her, because from where I was sitting it was clear that he did. She wasn't even pretty. And her clothes – she was like no one I'd ever go near at school, let alone be friends with. But I could see that there was something about her that held Ifan, hooked him in. Perhaps it was just that she was different. Perhaps that's all it was.

"So you here with your family?" I said.

Alys nodded, and looked out of the window again. "Yeah."

"So you got any brothers and sisters?"

"Yeah. A brother and a sister. Twins. Way younger than me. My brother drives me mad asking questions all the time."

"How old?" I asked.

"They're only five, so you know, that's just how it is."

There was silence for a few minutes.

"So how old are you?" I asked, to try and break the quiet. It was feeling really awkward in the car with this girl we hardly knew. I wished I hadn't agreed to come.

"Seventeen," Alys said, and then Marko butted in.

"Seriously, Hannah, you asked enough questions?" He leaned forward from where he was sitting next to me in the back and nestled in between the two seats at the front of the car. "Let's get some music on."

"Yeah, Hannah!" Alys said, turning on the radio. "You're starting to sound like my brother with all the questions!" And then the music came on and Alys turned it up louder. "I love this song!" she said and she almost squealed, and she looked at Ifan, and he laughed, and then together they laughed, and I just didn't get it – I didn't get what they were both so happy about. And then

Alys started to sing along to the song, and her voice was really good, and Marko was still leaning forward so he was between her and Ifan and he was singing along now too, and I knew the song, but nothing would have made me want to sing, because I had this feeling like I was with two of my best friends in all the world, but I'd never felt so lonely – so stupidly lost and lonely – before.

Marko leaned back so he was properly next to me again in the car.

"I won't lie to you; I don't think we should be doing this," I whispered across to him, under the music.

"Yeah, so why not?" he said and he smiled.

I looked at him directly, my eyes holding onto his, because I wanted to grab him, grab his attention, and I didn't know how else to do it but with my eyes.

"We don't even know her. She's a complete stranger. She's weird – odd. She's not like us. And I have no idea where we are. Enough reasons for you?"

"Come on, Hannah. I'm having a good time, aren't you?" Marko said, and then he pulled this face he pulls that always makes me lose it and I couldn't help but laugh.

And then he looked over at Alys and said, "Oh turn this one up, Alys. Love this song. And this one is for you! For us! For today!" And suddenly the feeling I'd had, of Marko making me feel better had gone, and I was left thinking only about how much he and Ifan seemed to like Alys. Right now they seemed to like her way more than me.

"It's just up here. Pull over and park by those trees," Alys said.

"Here? But we're in the middle of nowhere," I said, and no one answered me – they all just got out of the car. I waited for a moment and then I got out too.

"It's up this path," Alys said, walking fast, ahead.

Marko and Ifan followed and I fell in behind. It was scrubby and steep on the path as we walked, and all I could smell was the outside-ness, the alien other of it all. The only living things here as far as I could see were the birds, giant ones, circling against the heavy white sky. There wasn't even a hint of blue. It was all cloud. And there was so much of it you could almost feel it pressing down on you. We'd driven up these twisting single-track roads, crossed gates and grids to get to where we were, and it was high here. Really high.

"How far is it to the lake?" I asked. It didn't matter that I'd grown up in Harlech my whole entire life, I wasn't used to coming out into the middle of nowhere in the mountains like this. It just wasn't what we did – not with my friends, not with my family, not with anyone. It's what the tourists did, the walkers. Not us.

"Not far now!" Alys shouted back, without looking, and we all followed on for a few more minutes until we were standing next to Alys on a cliff edge, out of breath, looking out at a still and vast lake, all of us cloaked in that moment, in our silence.

"It's like we've stepped back in time," Ifan said eventually, and I knew what he meant. There was a low mist clinging to the water on the other side of the lake, and it felt like there was no wind here. No movement at all.

"I seriously feel like I'm in Jurassic Park or something," Marko said.

"It's amazing," Ifan said. He looked over at Alys. He was smiling. She smiled back at him. I wasn't sure if he was talking about the lake or her, but it was probably both, and all I wanted to do now was puke and get the hell out of there and go home.

We carried on standing together in a line, in silence, and it all felt seriously awkward. I mean, what were we going to do now? What was the plan? To just stand there and admire the view? I leaned forward slightly. The edge we were standing on was an overhang. There were rocks and crags below. I didn't like how high up we were. I didn't like how far down it was to the water. I reached into my bag to try and find my phone, to see if I had any messages. Maybe take a picture. Do something, rather than just stand there in some stupid line looking out at a stupid misty lake. And then Ifan's voice – suddenly shouting out – booming across the lake –

"Hello, Alys!"

– and then it rumbled back in an echo that seemed to glide around us, and all I could think was how Ifan really should have been playing it more cool. He seriously needed to be calmer than this if he was going to be in with a chance with Alys.

Except then, suddenly, there was her voice shouting back at him –

"Hello, Ifan!"

– and she laughed and looked over at him and he smiled, and I thought I could see the love hearts where the pupils of his eyes should have been. It was ridiculous.

I pulled my phone out of my bag and looked at my messages. Nothing. No signal. Of course. We were way up high in the middle of this freakin' nowhere place.

I looked up to see what Marko was doing. He was standing just behind Ifan and Alys and he'd picked up a rock. He was moving it from hand to hand, like he was weighing up whether to throw it over the edge or not.

"Dare you!" I said, putting my phone away, and he looked over at me and grinned, but before he could answer we were both suddenly completely distracted by Alys, who had crossed her arms in front of her and started pulling off her top.

The grin dropped from Marko's face, and he looked from her to me, but I couldn't look back at him, not properly, because I couldn't stop staring at Alys, who was continuing to undress. She stood there now in only a vest top and bra with a pair of boyish knickers, and I couldn't get over how tiny she was. She literally looked like a baby bird, her teeny little bones just about holding her skinny body together.

"Come on!" she said. "Let's jump!"

I heard what she said, but I didn't immediately react, because I was staring at her ribs now, jutting out from beneath her vest, and the strap of her bra, which kept slipping over the arch of her left shoulder. She looked like a kid. She'd said she was seventeen, but she looked just like a little kid.

"Jump?" Marko said.

"No way!" Ifan said, smiling. "Are you serious?"

"Yeah!" Alys said. "Totally serious. We're going to

swim! This is how we get in to swim. We jump! It's all part of the fun." She walked to the edge of the rock overhanging the cliff.

I looked across at Marko. Surely he wasn't going to do this. Surely he wasn't. This was madness. We were so high up. There were rocks and cliffs all the way down, and then the water. I looked over at Ifan. He was pulling off his hoody like he was going to follow.

"Seriously, guys…" I said.

I didn't know what I was going to say next, but I felt like I needed to say something, I needed to stop whatever was about to happen from happening.

Marko ignored me.

He turned and threw the rock he'd been playing with out in front of him and over the cliff edge. It was an exaggerated throw, his whole body seemed to go into it, his back arching with the movement, and the rock went out pretty far before it sank through the air, and was gone. I didn't hear it hit the water.

Ifan was taking off his tracksuit bottoms now.

"Seriously, Ifan. This is a really stupid idea. You're not actually going to do it, are you?" I said, and I walked closer again to the cliff edge and looked over it. "It's really high. You can't jump off this. Look! Have you even looked? There are rocks, it's a sheer cliff!"

"I've done it before," Alys said. "It's totally fine." She looked at me. "Trust me."

Silence.

Alys turned away.

"Marko?" I said, turning towards him now. "You're not going to do it, are you?"

Marko shrugged and flicked off one of his trainers, and then the other, and started to undo the button on his shorts. "Why not?" he said. "If Ifan's in, then I'm in too." He grinned at Ifan.

"Good one," Ifan said. "I'm in!"

Alys was standing with her back to us all, right on the edge. Her toes hanging over the rock, curling and uncurling, as she looked out at the lake from where she stood, her hands almost rigid by her side.

I didn't know what to do.

Ifan and Marko were arsing around now, joking, pulling off the rest of their clothes until they were standing there in just their boxers and T-shirts.

Then they went quiet.

I didn't want to be the only one not to jump. I didn't want to be that person. I was never that person – the one that freaked out and didn't do stuff. Never. But I didn't want to jump. I just didn't. I couldn't. I didn't want to die. Not in the middle of this freakin' weird nowhere place.

Not with Alys. Not like this.

I could feel my heart banging in my chest now.

Marko and Ifan walked up and stood next to Alys on the edge, one on either side of her.

Trust me, she'd said. But why should we trust her? What reason had she given us to trust her?

I didn't want my friends to die.

What if they jumped and they died, their bodies all smashed up on the rocks, and I was the one here, alive, with no signal on my phone, no idea how to drive, and in the middle of nowhere.

I looked around me again.

I literally had no idea where I was. No idea at all. Not even a sense of what direction I'd walk in to get home, or to get down to them, once they'd jumped. I could have gone back and waited by the car, but I didn't want to be there on my own...

I flipped off one of my shoes, and then the other. I was going to have to do this – jump with them. I had no choice. I had to do it. I couldn't be left up here, the only one who didn't jump, alone.

I called out.

"Hang on!"

"So how we gonna do this?" Marko said, looking at Alys.

I didn't take my eyes off them as I struggled to undo the button on my jeans.

Alys turned her head to look at Marko. "We do it together," she said.

I wriggled, still watching, pulling at the ankles of my jeans now, trying to get my feet out.

"Shit," Ifan said. "It's high."

"Yeah," Alys said. "It is."

I lifted my sweatshirt over my head.

"You've done it before though?" Ifan said, and I could hear a slight tremor in his voice. He was panicking. I was panicking too. "You said you'd done it before, right?"

"I'll count to three," Alys said, "and then we go."

I don't want to do it. I don't want to do it. But I don't want to be the one who is left.

"One…"

I pulled off my vest-top.

"Two…"

I shivered, standing in my knickers and my bra, fiddling with my watch strap. I couldn't jump with this watch. It would get ruined. Mum would kill me. She would—

"Three…"

I looked up.

And they'd gone.

Silence.

I couldn't move.

I stood alone.

I waited.

And then I heard them.

Screams. Laughter. Screams.

I couldn't see anything but it didn't matter, because I could hear the sound of mad exhilaration, and it was repeating with the echo, reverberating all around. They hadn't waited...

I had to do it now. On my own. I thought I was going to be sick.

I couldn't do it.

I couldn't.

Marko – my friend, right? Ifan – my friend too. They'd left me up here – and they were okay – and that was good, but now what was I going to do? I was up here on my own...

I had to do it.

I had to jump.

I walked towards the edge, and looked over. I could see them below, like little animations, their movements only visible because of the ripples and splashes orbiting around them in the water. These were jerky, but happy movements... They seemed happy.

I wanted to shout down to them. I wanted to ask them what it was like, how it was, how they were. I wanted to tell them to look up, to watch me, to wait for me, but I couldn't. I was too scared. Suddenly I had no voice...

I took four big steps back from the edge.

I took a deep breath.

And I ran.

Fear.

Fear.

Fear.

I threw my body as far forward from the edge as I could and as my feet lifted from solid ground there was only space and nothing and me and the pumping sound of panic in my head and in my ears and the cold air on my skin and the goosebumps lifting, the soft hairs on my arms rising, as I was falling, falling, falling and the water was getting closer, darker, closer and I thought the landing would never come and then it did...

Smack!

The brutal slap of the water against my skin – the sound before the hit – the hurt – excruciating planes of it, across my back, my bottom, my thighs, and before I had time to gasp a full breath I was under. I was plunging down so deep into the water I wasn't sure I'd ever come up again – and the cold – biting me – my heart – in shock

– my head – full of pressure – the fall – all over me – and whatever air I took in before I went under – it was not enough – it couldn't be – it will never be enough – and then out of nowhere a sudden gush of sound and colour and I realize my head's above the water – it is – I'm above the water and I hurt like hell but I'm here – I'm in the lake – and I'm alive. Except now I'm splashing around, trying to stay above the surface, and my movements are slow…too slow…I'm not moving as fast as I want to, need to, to get out, to the side of the lake. I'm like a toy with a dying battery that won't make it across the room, and my chest is so tight, it's heaving for the air, for whole breaths that won't come, and inside I'm wound up with the panic that I might sink under again and lose what little fight I have, and the pain on my thighs, my whole body, it's still there, still aching…and I can taste the water as it slides in and out of my mouth and there's nothing I can do to stop it going in…

I look around me. I look for Marko, for Ifan, my eyes scanning the waterline as my mouth keeps dipping in and out of the water, and I spit and blow as best I can, breaths of air not water, breaths of air not water…but still I can't get away from the water seeping into my mouth… I am trying my best to move, to swim, but I'm shivering uncontrollably now, and gasping, gasping, and then I see them, way away. They are swimming towards the rocks at the far edge, they're in my sight, and I want to make it over to them, to the rocks. They're nearly there, nearly safe. But they didn't wait. They didn't wait for me, they didn't wait to see me jump, see me surface... They left me. They left me and followed Alys.

And as I begin to swim, finding a rhythm in the water, a movement that begins to calm me, and in its repetition calms my breath, I look for Marko and Ifan. I focus on getting to them, to reaching them on the shore, to keeping them in my sight, and yet all the time I am thinking about how they left me. They left me. And I will never be able to forget that they did.

I felt the shallows, the stones and mud beneath my toes, and I sunk my feet down, deep. I dug them into the wet ground and my body followed – legs, back, shoulders – collapsing like a run of falling dominoes. And I was shaking now from the shock, the pain, the slap of the water against my skin. I heaved myself up a little onto the gravel shore and tried to sit, because I needed to. But it hurt; I didn't know what to do with my body – how to rest, how to be.

I looked down at my skin. It was red, blotchy. There

was a shocking mark where I'd hit the water. It scared me. I guessed I didn't have any broken bones, but I hurt from the inside out and the outside in. I'd never known my body could hurt this much.

I turned and looked behind me for Marko and Ifan. They were standing by some trees, shivering, but they were laughing. They were happy. Alys was with them, talking to them. She looked happy too.

"Hey!" I called out. "Marko! Ifan!"

I had to shout because I couldn't move. I could hear the injury in my voice, the weakness. I was still shaking.

Marko looked up and over at me, and he started to walk towards me.

"Hey you!" he said as he got closer. "Amazing, wasn't it?"

"No!" I said.

"Didn't you feel like you were flying? Like you were actually flying?" Ifan said. They were all standing around me now, their feet in the water, while I tried to find a way to sit in the shallows, on the ground.

"Why don't you ask me if I'm alright?" I said, looking at Marko. I thought I might cry. I seriously didn't want to cry.

"What do you mean?" he said, and he laughed. "I feel like I'm on top of the world right now! I flew! I feel like

I could fly again now!" He raised his arms out and flapped them about and laughed again, and Alys laughed too.

"Do I look *okay* to you?" I said.

"What?" Marko said. "What do you mean?"

"I think I'm the most okay I've been ever," Ifan said. "I never thought I'd do it. I honestly never did. But I did – *we* did – we did it! Just look at it!" He turned towards the cliff. "We did *that*! We jumped off *that*!"

"Well I'm glad you are all so happy, but in case you haven't noticed I can't actually stand up right now. I hurt all over. Literally *all* over. I was totally freaked out up there and you all just went and jumped – without me! Didn't you see me? I nearly drowned!"

"We didn't think you were going to do it," Alys said. Her voice was flat, calm.

"Yeah," Ifan said. "It didn't seem like you were up for it." He looked at Alys and Marko for reassurance as he said it. The reassurance of the group. He always looked for that. I hated that he did.

"We weren't going to make you do it if you didn't want to," Alys said. "You seemed pretty scared."

"I *was* scared!" I said, and the tears were pricking at my eyes now.

"Look," Marko said. "I thought the same. I didn't think you wanted to do it, so we just, we just—"

"You just went!" I said and I could hear that I was shouting now, but I was shaking too. Uncontrollably shaking. "I can't believe you did it. That you went and you didn't wait for me; didn't look out for me, check that I was okay. That's what friends do, isn't it? I was checking for you! I was looking out for *you!*"

"Hannah, listen—"

"I am listening, Marko, and you seriously aren't saying sorry. None of you are."

"I'm not sure what I need to be sorry for," Alys said.

There was silence.

"I'm sorry, Hannah," Ifan said. "I thought we were all having a pretty amazing day, to be honest."

I dipped my head down, and felt the tears hot on my face. Ifan still wasn't really saying he was sorry. He made me feel like I'd ruined his happy day.

"Listen, Hannah. We should have waited. I'm sorry," Marko said and I could tell he felt really awkward, because he was shifting on his feet, but he sounded like he meant it at least. "We should get you your clothes, get you warm. You look really cold."

"Here," Alys said, and I looked up to see her stretching her hand out towards me. She was offering to help me up off the ground. I hesitated. I didn't want to take her hand. Not hers. "Come on," Alys said. "We should go. Get our clothes and head back to the car." I didn't move. Partly because I was scared to – the ache inside my body was still so intense – but partly because I hated her for making me feel like this. It was because of her I was feeling pain like this.

"Come on!" Alys said again, leaning down towards me now. "There's another place I want to show you all." And before I could say anything she grabbed my hand, and pulled me up to make me go with her. And as I walked alongside her, weak and bruised, with Marko and Ifan up ahead, wet and shivering, their boxers clinging to their damp skin, their shoulders hunched to try and keep in some warmth, I couldn't shake this feeling that Alys had brought us here today on purpose. She'd brought us here and put us all in danger, and she'd meant to do it. But why? Was it simply for the thrill?

THIS
SUMMER

CAIT

MONDAY

1

I walked into the kitchen. Mum was sitting at the table with her book, and she looked up and smiled at me as I came in. There was no sign of Johnny yet. Thank god.

"Sleep well?" Mum said.

"Yeah," I said, walking over to the kettle to flick it on. While I waited for it to boil, I looked out of the window and thought about how it had been at the beach yesterday. It had all been so strange when Hannah had arrived with the poster of Ceri Rees, saying it looked like this girl Alys they knew from last summer. Marko had looked at the poster, and said he could kind of see a resemblance, but clearly it wasn't the same girl. Ifan had gone all intense again, like he'd been at the party, and then he'd walked up the beach a little way with Hannah as she had to go to work. I watched them as they walked. They looked like there were arguing, but then Hannah had stopped and given Ifan a hug before she'd left him, and when he came back to us at the lifeguard hut he didn't mention anything about Alys or the poster again. Marko didn't say anything either. It was strange how Alys kept coming into things. But when I'd asked them about her before no one wanted to talk, so I didn't ask again.

The kettle clicked off.

"Tea?" I said, turning to look at Mum.

"I've had one thanks," Mum said, her head still in her book.

I nodded. I still felt pretty sleepy. I was sure it was from swimming in the sea, and also the fumble and fight to get in and out of the wetsuit. I hadn't done anything like that – I mean anything new – for ages. Not since Dad died. I guess that was because since then life had kind of been on hold. So swimming like I had yesterday, floating on my back, my body gently lifted from time to time by the waves passing beneath me, staring up at the sky, it had made me feel…well, more alive again. And when I got out of the water I'd ended up having to get Marko and Ifan to pull at the wetsuit, pull at each leg and peel it off me, while I sat on the sand, getting dragged along. We'd laughed about it – all of us – we'd really laughed. And I mean, I felt kind of embarrassed at the same time too, because I didn't want to look like a complete idiot in front of Marko, but I hadn't laughed that much in ages, not even with Jade and Mia. I think with Marko and Ifan, because they don't know me, don't know about Dad and what happened, I feel more free, like I can be a different me. A happier me.

"Johnny still asleep?" I asked, sitting down at the table while Mum stirred some sugar into my tea.

"No, he's gone into town to get us some more bread and milk and a newspaper. So, tell me, how was the beach party on Saturday? We haven't really had a chance to talk since then."

If we'd been at home Mum would have been all over it, asking me how the party had been.

I got my tea and went over to the table and sat down with her.

"Yeah, it was good," I said, lifting the mug to my lips.

"Good?" Mum said smiling, looking for more.

"Yes," I said. "Good."

"So you don't want to tell me about it?"

"No, I do – I mean, I *did*, when I got back, but you know—"

"What?"

"Well it's just not the same, with Johnny here."

Mum nodded again. "Look, I know it isn't…well, easy—"

"I hated seeing you lying together on the sofa like that when I came in."

I said it as I thought it. Suddenly I wanted her to know how I felt.

"I know," Mum said. "I saw that. I can see that it's... well, awkward." She paused for a moment before speaking again. "I don't know what to say, Cait. I mean, other than I'm trying my best."

"I know you are, Mum, and I am too, but I still miss Dad. I really miss him. It's hard being here with Johnny. I can't just pretend like this is all normal. It doesn't *feel* normal to me."

"Cait, I want to be here and spend time with you, you know that, don't you? But you make it really hard for me when you don't want to do anything with Johnny. I'm stuck between you both. And I really want this holiday to work. We need this break."

I didn't say anything. I didn't know what Mum meant about needing a break. A break from what? It wouldn't matter if we went to the end of the world and back again, losing Dad would always be there. Always. I didn't understand how Mum couldn't see that; how Mum couldn't see how hard it was for me to enjoy almost anything at all since Dad had gone. Did she not feel the same way too?

The front door clicked open.

"Hi! I'm back!"

Johnny's voice in the hall.

It reminded me that these days, even when we tried to talk, Mum and I could never finish a conversation. Not on our own. Even when we were at home in London, Johnny was always ringing or texting her about something, or turning up and just being there.

I stood up.

"Hi!" Mum shouted back to Johnny, but then she stood up and pulled me in for a hug. And I let her hug me – it felt good. But as soon as Johnny came into the kitchen she let me go again.

"I think I'll head out this morning," I said. "For a walk." I picked up my mug of tea.

Johnny nodded. "Good, good."

Mum stepped forward and took the shopping bag from him. "Do you want tea, honey? Kettle's just boiled."

"Lovely," Johnny said.

And I left the room.

I went upstairs, and I got ready to go out, even though I had no idea where I would go.

When I came downstairs I pulled my walking boots out of the bag in the hall, shoved them on, and headed out. I guessed if I walked through the fields to the cove, the way Marko had taken me on Saturday night, and kept walking, I might eventually make it round the coast and onto Harlech Beach. It was worth a try, and if I did make it, Marko or Ifan might even be at the Coffee Shack or the lifeguard hut. I could maybe see them, get myself something to eat and drink. It was something to do anyway, so I could avoid spending time with Mum and Johnny.

The vast white sky, the mountains. That's all I could see as I walked through the first field – and the space – there was just so much space. I thought about Dad. It didn't feel right. It *wasn't* right that this was all still here, all of it, and he wasn't. I missed him so much, and I hated the feeling of missing him. But at the same time part of me wanted to keep missing him – needed to keep missing him like I did – so that in some way I kept him alive.

My phone buzzed in my pocket. I reached for it quickly. Surprised I'd got a signal out here. I stopped where I was and looked at the screen.

Hi. Are you in town? Want to meet for lunch?
I've just finished my shift. I've got an hour before
I'm back on again...

Marko. I'd forgotten that we'd swapped numbers at the party. Remembering that, and realizing I'd forgotten, made me think I must have been more drunk than I'd thought.

I replied straight back.

I'm about ten minutes from the cottage. Will head back and see if Mum can drive me into town. Will be quick as I can. Text you when I'm in.

I wasn't sure how to sign off. Did I put my usual kiss? I didn't, but it felt kind of incomplete not putting it there somehow.

I turned away from the estuary and headed back towards the cottages, and as I did I felt a little lift – a sense of feeling better, almost instantly. I didn't usually make decisions this positively, this quickly, not these days anyway. But I liked the thought of meeting Marko instead of being on my own on this walk. Now all I had to do was persuade Mum or Johnny to drive me into town.

As Johnny pulled into the car park by the castle to let me get out, I suddenly felt bad. I'd wanted to tell Mum that I hated his guts when we were talking this morning, and now he was totally helping me out, taking me into town so I could meet Marko for lunch. Admittedly he'd made seriously dull conversation in the car on the way, about the geography of the mountains, spouting all sorts of facts about Snowdonia, but I could tell he was really trying.

"Thanks for the lift," I said, smiling, getting out of the car, closing the door behind me. Johnny smiled back.

"No problem," he said through the window. "Have a nice time. Don't freeze in the wind!"

I smiled again and nodded.

Maybe I needed to try a little harder too.

"You want the paper?" he said, picking it up from the floor of the car and gesturing it towards me. "Must have fallen out of the bag this morning. Your mum and I are going out for the day now. I'm not going to read it – here, you have it."

I went to say no, but then I saw the headline: *Fears Remain for Missing Girl, Ceri.*

"Actually, I might take it. In case I have to hang around and wait for Marko," I said.

"Sure," Johnny said, and he passed it through the window to me. "See you later." And he was gone.

I stood where he'd left me on the edge of the high street and looked down at the paper. Ceri Rees's face stared back at me from the front page.

"'The family thought she'd be home by now. We all did. It's such a worry, not knowing if she's safe.'"

That was a quote from one of Ceri Rees's neighbours, who said she'd gone missing several times before over the last couple of years, but that she had always returned home within forty-eight hours.

I read on.

"'Ceri has been missing for over five days and we are extremely concerned about her whereabouts.'"

The police. It was clear they were beginning to think the worst.

I scanned the rest of the report. There was a number to call for anyone who might have any information on

Ceri, and then a quote from Ceri's stepfather. The paper said she'd been living with him since the death of her mother. It said the stepfather was concerned about Ceri; he had been since she'd lost her mum. He just wanted her to come home.

I looked at the photograph again.

She was seventeen. Older than me by a year, and yet somehow she looked younger. When I'd first seen her face on the posters at the weekend, all I'd thought about was how awful it was for her family to not know where she was, to be searching for her like they were. But now, reading this report, and hearing about Ceri losing her mum, I felt a different sort of a pull. A stronger one. For her. For Ceri. Because I knew what it was like to lose a parent. It was hideous. There was really no other way to describe it.

Suddenly I felt a hand, heavy on my shoulder.

I turned.

Marko.

He was standing behind me.

"Are you coming to the cafe, then?" he said, smiling, and with that smile I was jolted out of my sadness, out of thinking about Ceri. I found myself smiling back.

"Yeah, sure," I said and I folded the paper up, keeping it in my hand, because I was glad Johnny had given it to me now. I was glad somehow to have Ceri's story close by. Although I wasn't sure I could explain why I felt like that. Not even to myself.

As soon as we walked into the cafe I saw Hannah and Ifan sitting together over by the window.

Marko turned towards me. "I didn't realize they'd be in here," he said, and it felt like he was almost apologizing, but then he started walking towards their table, so I followed.

"Hey," Marko said as he reached them. "Okay if we join you?"

From the look on Hannah's face it was clear that she was pretty gutted that we were there.

"Course," Ifan said. "Sit down."

We sat, Marko opposite me, and I put the newspaper on the table in front of me, my bag on the floor.

I looked at Hannah. She seemed really distracted. It was strange that now I'd got to know her a little bit, she was actually nothing like the girl I'd thought she was when I'd first seen her in the deli.

"So I'll go and get us all coffees, yeah?" Ifan said, standing up, shuffling behind Marko's chair.

"Great," Marko said, shoving a tenner over his shoulder into Ifan's hand. "I'll have black coffee and one of those ham and cheese toasties." Marko looked at me. "What do you want?"

"Toastie sounds good," I said. "I'll have the same, and white coffee. Thanks."

"Nothing for me," Hannah said, and she flashed Ifan a short little smile before he went up to order.

"Good day?" I said, trying to make things feel a little easier while we waited for Ifan to come back.

"Fine," Hannah said. "You?" And she looked at Marko rather than me as she said it, and Marko gabbled on about how it had been pretty quiet so far at the beach, and I sat and listened, feeling like the complete outsider that I was. And then, thankfully, Ifan came back with the drinks and something somehow eased again. It was only Hannah who seemed to have a problem with me being there. I had no idea why. I'd done nothing but be nice to her since I'd arrived.

I took a sip of my coffee and looked up. Hannah was staring at me.

"Cait, can you take your paper off the table?" she said. "That picture is kind of freaking me out."

I looked at the image of Ceri's face again, large, staring back at me, staring back at us all now.

"Sure, sorry," I said, and I stuffed it into my bag.

Sometimes I hated myself for how eager I was to please.

There was silence.

"Actually, Cait," Ifan said, "I think you should get it back out."

Hannah looked at Ifan. She seemed angry suddenly.

"I think Marko should look at the picture again," Ifan said, glancing over at him.

Marko turned to me and he shrugged, so I leaned down and pulled the paper back out of my bag, putting it on the table in front of him.

"The more I look at it, Marko, the more I think Hannah is right," Ifan said. "I think it's Alys. I really do."

Hannah looked at Marko, and Marko looked at her. Was it for reassurance, or something else? I couldn't tell. Maybe there was more between them than I'd realized. Maybe I'd walked smack bang into the middle of some *thing* that they had. It would explain why Hannah was acting like she was. I'd only been here three days, so I knew nothing about what went on between them all, but there must have been stuff that went on. There's always stuff between friends.

I looked down at the picture of Ceri again. It was grainy, black and white, but that was because of the print. I could see it was a school photo. In colour it would have been bright. Ceri had that *I'm trying to look my best* smile that all school photos have and never quite pull off. Her hair was tied back in a ponytail. She was wearing a shirt, a blazer – her uniform.

"I'm not sure. I mean Alys was seventeen last summer – she must be eighteen now," Marko said. "This girl looks like she's about fourteen or fifteen."

"I wish I'd never said anything about it looking like Alys now," Hannah said. "I think we should just forget it, okay?"

"Why are you saying that, Hannah? I think you're right. It's her. It's just an old photo," Ifan said.

"But if your daughter went missing you wouldn't give the police and all the papers an old photo, would you?" Marko said. "You'd get something recent, show what she looks like now, so you'd have the best chance of finding her."

"I know this doesn't have anything to do with me," I said, butting in, "but it's Ceri's stepdad who's talking to the police. It says in the paper that her mother died. Maybe there isn't a recent photo. I mean, maybe a stepdad just wouldn't have a recent photo to give to the police?"

Hannah and Marko and Ifan all looked at me.

No one spoke.

And I wished more than anything that I hadn't opened my stupid mouth.

"I mean, I don't know…" I said, trying to cover up the silence and my stupidity. "I mean, no one knows, do they, about different people and different families and—"

"Yeah, well I guess that's kind of possible…" Hannah said, interrupting me. I was relieved that she had, and that maybe she agreed. "But what about her actual dad, and her friends?"

"Yeah, her friends would have photos on their phones. There'd be a recent photo somewhere," Marko said.

I thought about how, after Dad died, I didn't go anywhere or see anyone for months. I just got through each hour of each day and came home. That's just how it was. And if Mum died I knew it would be the same. Except maybe now I'd be left with Johnny. And if that happened, and I was left like that, and it was just Johnny and me, we wouldn't go out, do stuff together, take photos. You've got to get on with the people you're left with – want to be with them. You've got to be in a good place to do stuff like that.

"Maybe her dad just isn't around," I said, and as I said it I heard my voice kind of crack, and I was surprised by how I suddenly felt so much, when I actually hadn't said that much at all. "I mean, my dad died not that long ago, and I don't know anything about Ceri's stepdad or how long he's been on the scene, or where her real dad is, you know, but sometimes things aren't always as, well... straightforward as they seem."

It was quiet around the table, and Hannah, Ifan and Marko shared a look with each other. I couldn't tell if it was embarrassment at what I'd just said, or something else. I hadn't meant to tell them about Dad, but the words had just kept coming, and all I kept thinking about was Ceri Rees and how she'd lost her mum, and how she didn't seem to have a dad, and how once you've lost one parent you can't afford to lose another.

"I'm sorry," Marko said. "I'm really sorry about your dad."

I nodded because I couldn't, I didn't, want to say any more.

"But the thing is," Marko said, "Alys had a family. She talked about her mum and her dad. She had a sister and a little brother too, twins, remember?"

Ifan and Hannah didn't say anything.

Marko looked at Ifan.

"You had Alys's number, didn't you, Ifan? Have you tried it recently?" Marko asked.

"I've tried it loads," Ifan said. "I just get a dead tone. Nothing. It was like that after she left last summer. It's still the same now."

I glanced across at Ifan. He looked kind of desperate. Had something happened with him and Alys? He seemed really stressed not to have heard from her, and yet convinced now that the picture on the posters and the papers was her. Hannah seemed to think the same, although now she was completely backing off, which was just so weird after she'd bowled up at the beach and shown everyone the poster to start with.

"So none of you have heard from Alys since last summer?" I asked.

"Cait, I'm sure you're trying to help and everything, but you should just stay out of it, okay?" Hannah said, looking at me more directly than she ever had before. "You don't understand, because you can't. You weren't here last summer."

She paused for a moment, taking in a breath, and then she looked at Ifan.

"I think Alys is best forgotten, Ifan," Hannah said. "I'm sorry I showed you the poster. I shouldn't have. It's just…I saw a resemblance and I acted on it. I was scared. But I've thought about it and I think she's best forgotten. All I want to do is forget her."

"But *I* can't forget her," Ifan said. "I can't and I won't!"

It was suddenly quiet. I felt awkward again, like some kind of intruder in the group. The way Hannah talked to me had made me feel so small, like there wasn't a place for me here, and I just didn't understand what her problem was with Alys. What had happened last summer? Whatever it was no one seemed to be saying.

"I'm sorry," I said, quietly, but only to fill the silence and create some peace. It's what I always say in awkward situations like this.

"Don't be sorry, Cait," Marko said. "What are you even sorry for? Last summer, meeting Alys, it was kind of —"

"It was kind of insane," Hannah said. "Alys was insane, and Ifan, you are just as insane to still feel the way you feel about her now, to still talk about her like you do. She's not worth it, I swear—"

"Hang on, Hannah," Marko said. "Don't have a go at everyone now, especially not at Cait. She wasn't even here last summer. And so what if Ifan liked Alys? So what if he still does? You can't hold that against him. When you like a person, you like them. You can't stop liking them, however much you try…you can't control something like that."

I thought about what Marko was saying. I knew exactly what he meant. I'd been thinking a lot about him since we'd met. I didn't think I was really in control of that.

"You both seem to have conveniently forgotten that Alys clearly had a death wish," Hannah said. "She nearly got herself killed, and took all of us with her, and since the day at the lake none of us have heard from her. I don't think it's in any way normal to *like* a person like that, to think *romantically* about a person like that. I don't want to think about her *ever* again. But I do think this is her face – on the posters, in the papers – and I wish I'd never said anything now, but I have. So, if you both want to go on discussing it, or you want to do something about it, then I think you should go to the police. Let them deal with it. Because there's a girl missing, and that's big, it's serious, and so even if we don't have very much to tell them, it's probably the right thing to do."

"No! No way!" Ifan said.

"Why?" Marko asked. "What harm would it do? Surely if she's in danger – this girl – which she might be, you'd want to help her, Ifan, wouldn't you?"

I thought about the report that said that Ceri Rees had last been seen talking to a man in a blue car on the A496. I butted in.

"I know it's got nothing to do with me, but Ceri has been gone for almost six days now. The police have said they're extremely concerned. What if someone's taken her; is hurting her? It doesn't matter who she is – isn't it better to tell the police what you think you know, Ifan? Surely Hannah is right."

"No!" Ifan said, shaking his head, looking down at the table. "That isn't what we should do. Don't push me to do something that I…that I can't do. I'm sorry that none of you understand, but you can't understand, you won't—"

"So try and *make* us understand, Ifan!" Hannah said. "Because we all know you can't forget Alys, that you've tried to get hold of her, that you can't reach her, that you're going mad thinking about her, but look!" Hannah said grabbing the paper off the table, holding it up, pushing Ceri's picture in front of him. "She seems to have come back! She seems to be in trouble. And you're saying you won't do anything about it! Why? It doesn't make sense!"

Hannah paused, waiting for Ifan to speak, but he didn't.

There was silence.

I waited.

I didn't dare say another thing.

"So if you won't go, then I will!" Hannah said suddenly. "I'll do what Marko and Cait clearly agree I should do. I'll go to the police and tell them that we recognize this person; that we know her, that we met her last summer and she nearly got us all killed with her crazy daytrip into the mountains. And I'll tell them that this girl isn't Ceri Rees. Not to us. I'll tell them that this girl is Alys!"

PART
FOUR

LAST
SUMMER

IFAN

AT THE LAKE

I looked over at her. I couldn't help looking. Each time I glanced, taking my eyes off the road for a moment as I drove, I saw something new – some detail of her – her skin, her arms, her tiny wrists. A flash of her. Alys. And I liked it all. I liked all of her. And that feeling of liking all of someone – it was new.

"It's not far now," she said. "We have to drive right round the lake, so just keep going, keep following the road."

I nodded, glancing over, stealing another look.

"So how are you feeling?" she said. "After the big jump?"

Every bit of me was tingling, buzzing. I guessed it was the cold, the shock of the water on my skin still somehow clinging to me – except this didn't feel like shock. It felt like the biggest high. I was so high I wanted to scream.

"I feel amazing!" I shouted, as I drove, leaning forward

over the steering wheel, closer to the windscreen, like I was trying to tell the world. "I feel amazing!" I said again. I didn't have the words to say it any other way. I often didn't have the right words to say.

"Slow down, Ifan!"

Hannah's voice came from the back of the car, sharp, breaking the joy. Her mood hadn't changed one bit since we'd left the lakeshore. Alys had led us along this winding path through the trees back to the car, and then Hannah had stayed there while the rest of us went back up the path to find our clothes at the top of the cliff. Hannah might have stopped going on about how cold she was, but she was still off on one, moaning.

I looked quickly across at Alys again as I drove. She was smiling.

"I feel amazing!" I shouted again, my eyes on the road, and then I laughed and Alys was laughing too, and then I heard Marko's voice join us, and then he howled, like a wolf, and it was so random, but it was so right, that I joined him and did it too.

"I can't believe we just did that," Marko said. "We did it! We just jumped off *that*!" He pointed to the cliff through the car window. We could see it clearly now that we were on the other side of the lake. It was huge.

Alys screamed again and Marko screamed too and

I smiled, because I'd never felt so free and so happy and so completely *with* the people I was with before. I was so completely with Marko and Alys now. We were here together, doing the same thing, feeling the same thing. And then the screams broke down into laughter again, and I stretched out my arm towards Alys and placed my hand on her arm, just over her wrist, and I squeezed. I quickly looked across at her. I was suddenly anxious that I shouldn't have reached out and touched her like that. But she was laughing, still smiling at me, and any doubt I'd had just vanished. It was fine that I'd touched her. It had been clumsy and I didn't really know what I was doing, or why I was doing it, but it was fine. And I felt fine. I felt more than fine, in fact.

"There should be a clearing coming up, just after this bend," Alys said. "Slow down so you can pull in as soon as you see it."

I looked in the rear-view mirror to check there was nothing behind me, and saw Hannah. She was staring out of the window at the cliff, her face kind of pale, her hands pressed against her ears. It looked like she was trying to block us all out. Her eyes were squeezed shut. What was she doing – trying to block out our noise and the cliff and everything? It looked like she was. And that was weird because she was the adventurous one. She was usually the one right in the middle of things. She was the one who made stuff happen. But today it wasn't her in the middle of things. It was me. Alys and me. Today it felt like it was totally about Alys and me.

"There it is!" Alys said, pointing ahead, and I quickly pulled off the road and braked sharply, swerving into a little clearing that opened up in front of us just between the trees, with a shingle shore leading down to the lake.

"Careful, Ifan!" Hannah said.

She was in a right mood now. That was clear. And I knew Hannah well enough to know that her moods were hard to shift.

Alys got out of the car and started to walk towards the water. I followed, and Marko did too. She pulled off my hoody – the one she'd borrowed after our jump – and dropped it on the shingle as she walked, flipping off her shoes, leaving a trail of stuff behind her. I didn't care about my hoody. I was glad she'd borrowed it. I liked that she had.

"We'll get into the water here and swim out, head for those trees by the rocks," she said, pointing, still walking. "Follow me."

I looked at Marko. I'm not sure why I did that. I was used to checking in with him, following him whenever he was around. I didn't need to do that now. I wanted to go with Alys. I knew that. I wanted to go where she was going. I didn't need to check with Marko or anyone.

"What's she doing now?"

I looked around. Hannah had got out of the car and was standing a little way behind us on the shingle.

"Seriously, Marko. What are we meant to be doing?" Hannah said.

I kicked off my shoes. I was going to follow Alys into the water. I didn't care what Hannah thought.

"I don't know, Hannah, but let's find out," Marko said. I could tell he was being patient, trying to calm her down.

"You're actually up for another adventure? Are you serious? Wasn't the death jump enough for you?" Hannah said.

"What do you mean?" Marko replied. I could tell he was getting annoyed with her now too.

"Come on, Hannah!" I shouted over my shoulder, louder than I meant to, as I pulled off my tracksuit bottoms. I turned to look at her. "You're the one who always says I'm too shy, too quiet, no spirit of adventure. I'm going in. Come too!"

Hannah looked right at me. "No way, Ifan. No way."

I turned away from her and faced the lake. Alys was in the water now, swimming out towards the middle. I didn't want to lose her, be too far behind. I could hear

Hannah grumbling, her voice low. Marko was trying to persuade her to come into the water and she was refusing.

I didn't take my eyes off Alys.

"I'm going to wait for you here –" Hannah was shouting over to me at the water's edge – "with the car and all the stuff…the clothes."

"Okay, whatever," I said, and I started to wade into the water, without looking back. I was going to swim with Alys. I was going to do it, no matter what Hannah thought.

"Hang on, will you, Ifan? Wait for me," Marko said, and I could hear him coming towards me, the sound of his feet on the shingle behind me as I waded out, but I kept on wading. I didn't want to hang on, not even for Marko. And once I was up to my waist I pushed myself under the water, into the depths of the green darkness below. I felt the sharp ache of its cold on my skin, until I pushed my head up for some air.

I swam on. I had to, to keep warm, and I wondered as I swam, if Marko was behind me in the water.

I hoped he wasn't.

I hoped Marko had stayed with Hannah, because if no one stayed with her now we'd all suffer for it later.

It was Hannah who'd always told me I needed to come out of myself, live a little, be brave, and that's what I was doing today. Today I was brave. And feeling like this – meeting Alys, doing *this* – felt like the best thing I'd done in ages.

I kept swimming, my eyes on Alys, following her strokes with my own in the water. She was in the middle of the lake now. I didn't feel like I was that far behind, but it was hard to tell the distance across the water somehow, and the ache from the cold felt like it had moved from my skin to my muscles, to my bones – an ache that I hadn't really ever felt before. I turned and looked back to see how far I'd come, to see where Marko might be, but when I caught sight of him, he was still on the shore, crouched down next to Hannah, who was sitting on a rock, her head bowed. It looked like she was upset, like Marko was comforting her.

"Shit," I said under my breath, turning back towards Alys. I knew I should go back. Hannah was my friend. But I didn't want to. She had Marko, didn't she...? I wanted to be with Alys. I was pretty sure that if things had been the other way around Hannah wouldn't have come back for me... I turned and looked towards the shore again. I'd swum pretty far out. I was almost in the middle of the lake now. It made more sense to keep going than to turn back...

I swam on.

Alys was heading towards some rocks on the other side of the lake. I wanted to get to her, but the harder I tried to speed up, the slower I felt like I was going. I'm not a strong swimmer. Marko always takes the piss out of me for that. He tells me I'm like a slappy duck.

"Yeah, and you're best mates with this slappy duck," is what I always say back.

But seriously, right now, my speed, the push of my strokes, my style – if you could even call it that – were all horribly slappy duck, and I was getting nowhere. Trying to catch up with Alys now was only reminding me how bad I was at all this – swimming, being with a girl I liked, being totally myself...

A shout from up ahead.

"You coming?"

Alys was almost at the rocks now, treading water, facing me, waiting for me.

"Yeah!" I shouted back, and I could hear the rasp in my voice where my breath should have been.

I tried hard to contain my out-of-control limbs as I swam, and as I got alongside her, she started to swim on again. We were swimming together now towards the rocky shoreline, in silence, side by side. I'd made it. I hid my smile under the water as we went.

The water grew darker the closer we got to the rocks.

I looked up. We were beneath an overhang in the cliff face. It was stealing the light. It was sucking out any warmth we had left from our bodies moving in the water. I felt goosebumps rise and watched as Alys swam around three huge fallen rocks, creating a pathway of ripples for me to follow. They led towards a series of smaller rocks and some shingle where we could get out.

As I swam the final stretch, I watched Alys rise out of the water from the shallows in front of me, her body so tiny and yet so strong, the few clothes she was wearing – a bra, a vest, her knickers – stuck to her like a sheet of the finest tissue paper. It moulded to her, revealing the shape of her body. She was so confident, as if the way she was, the way she looked right now, was just how she was meant to be. It surprised me. How she looked. How I felt. Everything about her surprised me.

The water began to shallow around me, the ground harden beneath my feet. I bent my legs to stand. Was this a cave? It *felt* like a cave. I looked behind me and back out at the lake. There was no sign of Marko or Hannah. They must have both stayed by the car.

"Are you coming?" Alys said, and her voice almost echoed.

I walked clumsily towards her. She was sitting on a huge slab of grey rock, the top of it flat like a table, her knees pushed up to her chin so she was bunched up, small. I just wanted to get to her now.

"It's awesome in here," I said, climbing to sit next to her. Close, but not too close.

She nodded, looking up, and I looked up too. There was a great hollow above us, a thin shaft of light. Water dripped from it onto the rocks all around us, creating a shine against the wet slates. Everything glistened.

"It's like some kind of inside-out night sky," I said, and I looked over quickly at Alys, suddenly self-conscious because I'd said the exact thought that was inside my head.

Exposed.

That's how I felt.

"Do you want to kiss me?" she said, suddenly.

I looked at her.

Did she mean it?

I hoped she did, because I wanted to kiss her. I wanted to kiss her more than I'd wanted to do anything before in my life.

I leaned forward, slowly.

I kissed her.

And gently, she kissed me back.

And as her lips left mine I felt, just for that moment, as if I'd been somewhere else.

I'd never kissed anyone like this before. I wondered, had she?

"Was that okay?" I said.

Alys smiled.

"I mean did you want me to kiss you – like that?"

"I did," Alys said. "I really did."

I nodded and looked down at my feet. I shivered. I was cold. But I didn't want Alys to see that I was cold. I didn't want to ruin the moment.

"So how do you know about this place?" I said.

"My mum and dad used to bring me here," Alys said. "Before my brother and sister were born. We used to have picnics on the shore back where we left the car, and then my dad would swim with me out here to the cave. I used to think it was full of all sorts of terrible things."

"What sorts of things?"

"You know – monsters, ghouls, trolls."

"But now you know those don't exist any more," I said, and I smiled.

"Well, yeah, no – I don't know. I kind of think the monsters do still exist, it's just that they're different now."

I felt a weight descend as Alys spoke. It was like a mist had come in off the mountains, and was wrapping itself around us, smothering us like a blanket, here in the cave. She looked frightened – crushed.

"Different how?"

Alys was quiet. Suddenly I felt like I shouldn't have asked.

"You don't have to tell me…" I said.

She looked at me.

"Being alone," she said. "Losing everything. Not being loved. Those are my monsters now."

I put my arm around her and pulled her in so she was close to me, my hand on her back. I felt the curve of her shoulder blade. It sat perfectly in my palm like a shell I'd scooped up from the beach, her skin cold, as cold as mine. Together like this we seemed to fit.

I leaned in to kiss her again, to touch her, feel her lips again, the warmth of them on mine. She turned to me, and we kissed and we kissed, and as we kissed I couldn't believe that this girl I was holding now, kissing, was the same girl who'd screamed my name from the clifftop, who'd got me to jump, who'd sung and howled – because all her confidence, all her shout, seemed to have turned into a perfect kind of quiet in my arms.

"Tell me something that no one else knows about you," Alys said, pulling back, stretching out her legs in front of us on the rock. She wasn't looking at me. She was playing with a thin gold chain, a bracelet on her wrist that I hadn't noticed until now. It had a little gold-leaf charm hanging from it and she twisted it round and round while she waited for me to speak.

"What? Like a secret?" I said.

Alys nodded, still playing with the chain.

I looked at her pale hands, her fingers, the charm. I couldn't think of any secret I was keeping, or any secret I had ever kept, and certainly no secret that would have been interesting enough to tell her now. Life had been dull. Nothing had ever happened to me. I was just some local boy in a small town in North Wales, who'd always been too frightened, too shy, to do anything about anything, until today.

"Today..." I said, and then I lost my thread, my thinking, my confidence and I didn't go on. But what I wanted to say was that what had just happened with her, today, was perhaps the closest I might ever get to having a secret – something I'd keep close, not tell, something I'd treasure.

"Today?" Alys said, smiling.

I nodded. I couldn't read her smile. I was still struggling for the words, and I knew I sounded like an idiot, saying what I'd said and then not saying anything at all.

"Okay," Alys said. "Today!" And she repeated my word, confidently, like she understood, and in saying it she made my stupid word sound less stupid. She made it sound like she knew exactly what I had meant.

I looked up again, and Alys leaned in towards me and kissed me, slipping her hand into mine, leading it gently across her body to her waist. I felt the soft flesh and bones of her against my hand, and it was bliss to be with her, touching her like this.

She pulled gently away, her hand still clasped in mine.

"Now ask *me*," she said.

For a moment I still felt lost in her kiss, in her touch, but then I realized what she was asking.

"So tell me something that no one else knows about you, Alys."

Just saying her name felt nice.

Alys looked down at her right hip, and my gaze followed. Her fingers still interlaced in mine, she guided my hand from her waist down to her hip, glancing up at me as she lightly pulled at her vest, her knickers, not letting go of my hand. And there, on the curve of her hip bone, sat a tiny blue butterfly tattoo.

"No one," Alys said, looking straight at me, "knows about this, but you."

No words came into my head.

Without thinking, I bent down and I kissed her, there, on her hip, resting my lips gently on the tiny butterfly.

"Is that okay with you?" Alys said.

I nodded and I kissed her again, this time on the lips, and this time it felt stronger. It was so totally okay with me.

And then she pulled away, her hands holding me now – holding my arms – and she faced me where we sat on the rock.

"I need you to hold on to my secret, Ifan. Can you do that? Will you?"

"I…" I went to speak, but I was confused. I didn't really know what she was saying, what she meant.

"Can you keep my secret?" she said again.

I nodded. "Yes."

"Because I think it might help me – another time – another day – just knowing that you know."

"Are you okay, Alys? Are you in trouble? Is everything okay?"

I felt sick now. Sick that maybe she wasn't okay. Sick that this day would end, that somehow Alys – me – this – all this – might end – and she wouldn't be okay and I'd never know.

She grabbed my hands in hers and she squeezed them tight.

"I'm okay," she said. "Right now, here with you, I'm totally okay."

I looked at her. Her eyes huge, searching mine. I had this feeling like she wanted something from me, something I didn't know how to give, and she wasn't going to let me go without it. She had me entirely in her grasp. I knew it, and she did too.

"You're not like me," she said. "Things always go wrong for me. But I can see that for you, it's different."

"I'm still not sure I know what you want," I said. "Is there something you want me to do?"

"Just hold on to my secret," Alys said. "And if something happens, and you're sure, really sure that it's the right thing to do, then let it go. You can let my secret go."

I looked at her. Her eyes. Dark brown. So dark I could have fallen into them and completely disappeared.

"I trust you," she said. She leaned in close to me. "Can you trust me back on this? Will you?"

I trusted her. I did. No one had ever had so much confidence in me before. And I liked her more than anything or anyone I knew.

I looked down again and brushed my fingers over the butterfly tattoo, transfixed by the blue. And I thought about how like a butterfly Alys was – how delicate and strange. I liked that there was stuff about Alys that only I knew.

I looked up.

"I can do it," I said. "I can keep your secret safe."

"I knew you would, Ifan. I think I knew as soon as I saw you," she said. "So from this day on my secret lies with you."

PART
FIVE

THIS
SUMMER

CAIT

TUESDAY

1

I walked into the kitchen. I needed tea.

"Hi, Mum…"

"Morning. You sleepy? Shall I put the kettle on?"

I nodded and managed a smile, going over to sit at the table with Johnny.

"You didn't come down from your room last night after you got in. Everything okay?"

I nodded. "Yeah, just tired."

"Nice day though? Were you with Marko?"

"Yeah, met some of his friends again from the party, then I went down to the beach for a bit and waited for him to finish his shift. We hung out, went for a swim."

Mum smiled. "Nice," she said, and then she went back to the kettle to make the tea.

I looked over at Johnny. He'd obviously got up bright and early because he already had his boring newspaper and had eaten all his boring muesli too. The radio was on.

Loud. Too loud. Stupid local radio playing rubbish rock songs. Just the sort that Johnny loved. I'd suffered enough of them on the journey up here. He had tons of CDs of it in his car. I couldn't face any more.

"Morning, Cait," Johnny said, his nose poking over the top of the paper.

I smiled. A fake smile, but still a smile. I guessed he wouldn't know the difference and just hoped that Mum didn't see as she came over and put the tea down in front of me.

"So, I was thinking it would be nice if we all did something together today," she said. "A walk, maybe? I've found a load of maps in the chest of drawers in the sitting room. Did you bring your boots, Cait?"

I nodded, picking up the tea and slurping a hot gulp. I had my boots but I wasn't going on a walk with Mum and Johnny. No way. What I wanted to do was see Marko. He was the first thing I'd thought about when I'd woken up, and the last thing I'd thought about before I'd fallen asleep last night. If I went down to the beach again today then I guessed I might see him. I thought about Hannah and Ifan. They might be there too. I wondered if Hannah had gone to the police in the end? I really wanted to know. She'd been so sure about going. I would definitely go to the beach today, I decided. I wanted to see Marko and I wanted to find out more about what happened after I'd left everyone yesterday.

The news suddenly came on the radio, interrupting my thoughts.

Harlech Beach has been closed since the early hours of this morning whilst Gwynedd Police, who are investigating the disappearance of missing girl Ceri Rees, search the beach and surrounding area. A statement is expected later on this morning. It is understood that a member of the public contacted the police after finding evidence in relation to the teenager's disappearance. Ceri was last seen speaking to a man in a blue car heading in the direction of Porthmadog on the A496 on Friday 8th August. At this stage it is unclear when the beach will be reopened. Police are asking the public to assist them in their operation by avoiding the area until further notice.

I stood up and my chair made an almighty screech as it scraped against the slate floor.

Mum and Johnny immediately looked up at me.

"I'm going to get ready, finish my tea in my room," I said.

"Come back when you're done and we'll look at the maps, plan where we might go," Mum said.

I didn't say anything. I went straight to my room and grabbed my phone and called Marko. I was suddenly desperate to talk to him. Was he at the beach? Was he there with the police? What if it was him who had found the evidence they were talking about on the news? There was no answer. I tapped out a text.

Hi. Are you at the beach?
Just heard the news. x

I put a kiss this time. I'm not sure why. Habit maybe. And because I was acting fast. Or maybe it was because I wanted to. We'd had a nice time just hanging out together yesterday.

I slung the phone onto the bed, and stopped for a moment to think about what I might do next.

"Cait?"

It was Mum. She was at my bedroom door.

"Can I come in?"

"Yes," I said.

Her head appeared, and then she came into the room, pushing the door shut behind her.

"Listen, are you okay?" she said.

"Yes," I said.

It came out wrong. Fast. Loud. Defensive. The word I'd said was *Yes* but the meaning was clearly *No*.

Mum walked over to me and put her hand in mine.

"Come here," she said, and she sat down on the bed, guiding me to sit down next to her.

"You seem like you're in a really bad mood," she said.

"I told you, I'm just tired," I said, more gently this time.

"Right," she said. "Yes. We're all tired, I think, but you know you're not making much of an effort with Johnny and he's feeling it."

I clenched my jaw shut, so my mouth didn't fall open into a massive gaping hole, so that all the angry words that were sitting inside it, all the words that were jostling, bustling, jockeying to come out and pack a punch, didn't get said. It would have been a knockout if I'd said them all. It would have been a bloodbath.

"The thing is, Cait," Mum said, "I can't put in all the effort for both of us. I need you to make an effort too. Johnny is really trying."

"I didn't even want to come on this stupid holiday!" I said. "And you knew that!"

"Did I?" Mum said.

"No! Yes! I was trying to tell you before we came!" I said. The hurt from what Mum was saying, how she was being, not understanding how I felt, stung all over. "Look, just because you like Johnny, it doesn't mean I have to."

"But I want you to like him, Cait. I really do. If you

gave him a chance I think you'd find that he's nice. And he'd really like to get to know you better."

I took a deep breath and nodded.

I wanted to explain to Mum that making friendships, or relationships, or whatever it was I was meant to be doing with Johnny now, had to be a two-way thing. Both people needed to want to do it. Surely she knew that? Just because Johnny wanted to get to know me, it didn't mean I had to want to get to know him. I didn't have to feel the same. And anyway, he only wanted to get to know me because of Mum, and so what did that really mean? It meant nothing.

"Look, Cait, the thing is, I want Johnny in my life. I love him, and he loves me, and I would like for you to be able to accept that."

"Well what if I can't!" I shouted. "Seriously, what if I can't!" I could feel all the hurt all the anger all the unfairness of what she was asking me to do, how she was asking me to be, swelling inside me like heat. Why did she love him? Why? I didn't want her to love him and I didn't want to lose control and I didn't want to cry, so I didn't. I swallowed my tears, my emotion, and all that came out was my anger.

"I hate him, Mum. I hate him! And I hate you for making us come here and try and play happy families like this. You might not think I'm trying, but I am. I really am. But I can't do it. I want Dad back, and if I can't have him back then I think I might have to just go somewhere else – because seriously I can't do this. I just can't."

I grabbed the clothes I'd been wearing last night from the floor, and my phone from the bed, and I went towards the door. I looked back at Mum. She was still sitting motionless on the bed.

"I'm going to the bathroom to get dressed," I said. "And I won't be coming on your walk today, Mum. You go with Johnny. You go with him!" I slammed the door shut.

Wasn't it enough to have lost my dad? Now I was losing my mum too.

2

I left the house and I went up the lane towards the road. I just wanted to walk. My head was full of angry upset thoughts, and once I started walking I just wanted to keep going. I didn't care where I was heading. And it wasn't long before I was on the main road to Harlech, with no pavement or footpath, the passing cars pushing me onto the slope of the verge. I suddenly wished I hadn't come this way. A lorry rattled past, full of sheep – shit and general sheep debris flew off the back of it as it went by, the driver honking his horn at me to get off the road. I was in serious danger of getting run over here. I climbed higher onto the verge but the ground was so uneven and the grass was long and dewy, my canvas beach shoes immediately lapped up the wet. Why was I even wearing these shoes?

I stopped walking. God, I hated this place. It was all so alien, so far away from London. Here I was, completely alone, stuck on some stupid wild Welsh road with a load of, well, nothing, except the cows and sheep, for company. I reached into my pocket for my phone, to see if there was anything from Marko. Nothing. I put the phone back in my pocket and kept walking on the edge of the road now, so I could actually see where I was putting my feet. I wasn't sure how long it would take me to get to Harlech this way. Probably ages. I'd always got a lift before. I looked at my phone again for the time. 11.07 a.m…

Another horn. A car passed me, fast. I felt a rush of air as it went by. It had been close. Too close. I stepped back onto the verge. My shoes were soaked through now. I looked up. Had the car slowed down? Had it stopped? It looked like it had… I kept walking, looking ahead all the time… It had definitely stopped. Its lights were flashing, and another car, coming up from behind it, was slowing to pass. Why was it stopping here, on the edge of the road? I looked again. It wasn't a car I recognized. It wasn't Mum or Johnny. Thank god.

I suddenly thought about Ceri Rees. She was last seen on a road like this one, on the other side of Harlech, talking to a man in a blue car… Was this what had happened to Ceri? Was this how it had happened? I felt panic rising in my chest, my throat. A blue car, and I was so close to it now, too close to stop walking, or to find another way, because there *was* no other way. I was trapped. Fields on my left, hedges – no fences or gates. It was the same on the other side of the road – there was nowhere to go… I looked closer. I couldn't quite see into the car, but it looked like there was a man in the driver's seat. Yes, it was definitely a man. I was going to have to walk on. I was going to have to walk on like everything was completely okay, reminding myself that there were other cars passing by occasionally. Maybe I could even flag someone down if I needed to… Was this what went through Ceri's head before she was taken, I wondered… I kept walking… I'll be confident, I said to myself, and I walked up to the car and clambered slightly higher up the verge to pass alongside it, scraping my clothes on the bushes as I did. I felt like such an idiot. How had I got myself into this?

"Get in!"

The man's voice came from inside the car.

I glanced down and could see his body leaning across the passenger seat.

I felt my breath catch in my throat.

Panic.

"I said, get in!"

His voice again.

I couldn't move.

I'd been so stupid. Stuck here between the car and the hedge. Unseen now. Panicking now. Shit.

"What the hell are you doing? Cait! Get in!"

He'd said my name.

He knew me.

I dipped down lower, to look into the car…

Marko.

It was Marko!

"What the hell? Seriously, Marko! What the hell!" I started to laugh, but it was relief and fear and more relief wrapped into one and I sounded like a mad person, and I thought for a moment I was going to laugh and cry all at once. "You freaked me out! I didn't know you had a car! I thought I was about to get taken, like Ceri Rees! Blue car, you know?"

"Cait! I thought it was you. Get in!" Marko said. "This is my dad's car! It's been in the garage all week. I just picked it up."

I got in the car. Marko looked at me. "What the hell are you doing walking along this road? Seriously, you could have got yourself killed."

"I – I just had to get away for a bit, go for a walk," I said. "But yeah, I realize now it was a stupid place for a walk. Really stupid."

I looked at Marko. I was so glad it was him in the car

– that I was here now with him.

"So have you heard the news?" he said, looking in his mirror, pulling back onto the road.

"Yeah, I tried to call you, I texted you. Did you get my message?"

Marko shook his head and carried on.

"I think Ifan is at the beach," he said. "That's why I'm heading down."

Marko looked stressed.

"You're worried about him, aren't you?" I said.

"I've tried his phone, but he's not answering. I mean that's not unlike him, but all this Alys stuff, the poster. He's kind of on the edge. He's convinced himself this missing girl is Alys."

"And what do you think?"

"I don't think it's her," Marko said, and he glanced over at me. "I really don't. I can kind of see how you might think that Alys looks like Ceri Rees in that one photo, but the picture isn't really clear enough, and all the details are wrong. Ifan and Hannah are thinking way too much about last summer and they're both freaking out. They're just not thinking straight."

"So what did happen last summer?"

I wanted to know. I was desperate to know and no one was telling me.

"Just a weird day with this strange girl who Ifan fell in love with and Hannah, I guess, well, hate's a strong word, but…well, if you can fall in hate, then I guess Hannah did with Alys."

I nodded, but Marko's answer still didn't really explain. I felt like he was playing it down, playing down whatever it was that happened, and it was beginning to feel almost maddening. I tried a different tack.

"So did Hannah go to the police yesterday?"

"No," Marko said. "She said she'd go this morning; that's what she was saying when we left each other last night anyway. We haven't spoken since then."

"You met Hannah last night? After I left you at the beach?"

"Yeah. To talk, you know?"

I knew it was stupid to feel left out. I hated myself for it, but I did. Was there something between Hannah and Marko that I'd missed? Maybe it was really obvious and I just hadn't seen it? Jealousy suddenly had a hold of me like a snake curling around my heart. It was a strange feeling, and it surprised me.

"You okay?" Marko said, looking over at me.

"Yeah," I nodded, pulling myself together, and I looked out at the road. I could see police and a cordon. It looked like there was a roadblock up ahead.

I was the newcomer. I had to remember that.

I was the new person in all this.

I didn't know anyone that well.

I hadn't been here last summer.

And I didn't know what happened, because I hadn't met Alys.

3

Marko parked up on the side of the main road just by the turning to the beach. There was a cordon right across the turning, and police all around.

"Are you okay to wait in the car? I just want to see if they'll let me through first."

"Sure," I said, looking again at the scene in front of me. There were police dogs, searchers. So many people standing around. I watched Marko walk up to one of the officers. It looked like he was trying to persuade him – arguing that he needed to go down onto the beach as he was one of the local lifeguards or something. It was clear he really wanted to see Ifan. He was doing whatever he could to get past.

I pulled my phone out of my bag.

I wondered if there'd be any news online about the search.

I typed in: *Ceri Rees missing North Wales*

All the recent headlines flew up onto my screen – the reports about Ceri, her picture. There was nothing there that I hadn't already seen. I continued scrolling down. More of the same. And then a different headline...about a fatal traffic accident...a car crash on the Barmouth Road...a woman, Maddie Rees-Roberts, and her eleven-year-old stepdaughter Mariam Roberts both killed, pronounced dead at the scene... I kept reading...

Maddie Rees-Roberts's fifteen-year-old daughter, Ceri Rees, survived the accident and was treated for minor injuries...

Where was the date? When was this? I scrolled up to the top of the article. Two years ago. Ceri Rees had lost her mum two years ago. She'd lost her mum only six months before I'd lost my dad.

I looked up.

I remembered seeing Dad at the hospital. He was there for two days, in a critical condition, before he passed away. Two lost days. I sat with him, held his hand. I couldn't take my eyes off him, because he looked like my dad and not like my dad all at the same time. With his injuries and the medical stuff around him, attached to him, he was there, right in front of me, and yet he wasn't there at all. I think I knew then that I'd lost him.

I felt so angry and so sad when I remembered how it

had been, and then I thought about how angry and sad I still was. I wished I could get away from those feelings. I wished I could dump them somewhere behind some bins, just run away from them all.

I looked down at my phone again. What must it feel like to be Ceri? What must it feel like to have been there, in the crash, to lose your mum and your stepsister like that, in an instant? What must it feel like to have survived? Below the headline it said it was a miracle that Ceri had lived. But I couldn't see how anything that had happened to Ceri could be called a miracle at all.

Suddenly the car door opened and Marko got back in. It made me jump, but Marko didn't seem to notice.

"They won't let me onto the beach," he said. "They've closed the path."

I put my phone away.

"Did they say what's going on?"

Marko shook his head. "No. I guess we just have to wait."

I nodded.

There was silence.

It felt kind of awkward suddenly, Marko and me sitting there in the car, both staring out of the window, the police all around. I wasn't sure why, but I just couldn't think of a single thing to say.

"Listen," Marko said, saving us. "You don't have to wait here with me – unless, you know, you want to… I mean, you arrived here four days ago and walked right into the middle of all this, and somehow you've kind of, well, stuck—"

I looked at him.

"I mean that in a good way," he said quickly, and then laughing, "I mean it in a really good way." And then he looked at me. "But seriously, I'd understand if you just want to get back to your family, to your holiday. Everything happening here right now is such a mess."

I didn't speak. I wasn't sure what he was saying to me. And there were too many things that I wanted to tell him now. They were all jumping around one after the other like a bunch of frogs in my brain, and I couldn't make them stop, grasp one, show him, tell him.

I looked over at him.

I wanted him to know more about me.

I wanted to tell him about my dad, about what happened.

I wanted to tell him that I didn't feel like I had a family any more.

I wanted to tell him that in some small way I understood how Ceri Rees must feel.

And I wanted to tell him that I liked him.

And I wondered, if I just kept on not saying anything, and if we kept looking at each other like we were, whether maybe, just maybe, he might kiss me instead…

His phone rang.

"Shit," Marko said, scrambling around in his pockets to find it. "Sorry. I've got to get this, it might be Ifan…"

He pulled the phone out, and looked at me as he answered.

"Hannah," he said. "You okay? Have you heard from Ifan?"

I felt a pang of jealousy again, but I pushed it down and turned away from Marko, to look out of the window. I watched the police standing round the cordon. There were dogs, vans. It was hard to know how long this would all go on for.

"Yes, sure," Marko said. "I'll come now. See you there." He hung up.

4

As soon as Marko and I walked into the cafe I saw the look on Hannah's face. She wasn't happy to see me, and I had that feeling again that there was more between Hannah and Marko than they were letting on, but I was finding it all so hard to work out.

"She seems to go everywhere with you these days, Marko," Hannah said, and she smiled at me, but I recognized that smile. It was the same smile I'd given Johnny this morning at the kitchen table. The fake one. I'd thought he'd fallen for it, but there's no fooling anyone when you smile a smile like that.

"Hi, Hannah," I said. "You alright?"

Marko had said that Hannah as good as hated Alys. I was pretty sure that she hated me too right now.

"Well, not really," she said.

"So did you go to the police this morning?" Marko asked, sitting opposite her. I sat next to him.

"I went to the station, but they were all down at the beach. The officer at the desk took my name, my number, but told me to come back later. Said the detectives on the case were too busy right now, there was no one available for me to talk to."

"But that's mad," I said. "What if you had some information? I mean something vital – recent, like what if you'd seen her *now*?"

"Well, I know!" Hannah said. And she stared at me, her face pinched like an ugly scar. She was angry. I understood why. I hadn't meant it to sound like the information she wanted to take to the police wasn't relevant or important.

"It's a small place," Marko said. "Stuff like this doesn't happen round here very often. I guess they're just not set up for it when it does."

He was trying to smooth things over for Hannah. I'd noticed before that he could be kind like that.

I glanced over at the counter. I was hungry. Seriously hungry. I hadn't had any breakfast, and the smell of coffee and the sight of food was making my stomach grumble.

"So you didn't get hold of Ifan? You didn't speak to him?" Hannah said, looking at Marko.

"No," Marko said. "I went down to the beach because

he wasn't at home, and he's not answering his phone and I couldn't think where else he would be."

The radio was on in the cafe. It was the same rubbish local radio station Johnny had on at the cottage. Local radio seemed to be all anyone listened to around here. I wondered whether we might hear anything on the news about what was happening on the beach.

"It was hard to tell when they might reopen it, wasn't it, Marko?" I said. "Listen, do either of you want something to eat or drink? I'm happy to go up and get it."

Hannah didn't say anything for a moment. She looked at me, and then at Marko. "I know what's going on at the beach," she said.

"You do?" Marko said. "How? Why didn't you say?"

I could tell he was cross that Hannah hadn't said anything until now.

"Because I wanted to tell you face to face," Hannah said. "Ifan texted me."

"So he's there? He's definitely there?" Marko said.

Hannah nodded, pulling out her phone.

"He found some clothes. They were left in front of the lifeguard hut."

Hannah was clasping her phone tightly in her hand.

"So the evidence that's been found? That they reported on the news?" I said. "Was it Ifan who found it?"

Hannah nodded.

"Shit," Marko said. "Why didn't he pick up his phone and talk to me. Is he okay?"

Hannah looked at Marko.

"He said the clothes they found were Alys's. The ones she was wearing at the lake last summer." Hannah opened up her phone and showed us a photograph – a pile of clothes on the sand.

Marko looked at the picture. He didn't say anything.

"You have to admit, they look like Alys's," Hannah said. She seemed kind of desperate now, like Ifan had been before, waiting for Marko's response.

I looked at Marko. It was hard to tell what he was thinking. To me it looked like the clothes could be anyone's. And these were clothes she'd worn a year ago – would any of them really remember?

"I don't know," Marko said, looking at the picture, shaking his head. "It's hard to tell." He paused before speaking again. "So is Ifan sure? Really sure?"

"Look closer, Marko," Hannah said. "Look at the sweatshirt, that filthy sweatshirt, the vest, the jeans... Ifan says there's a rip in the sleeve. I borrowed that sweatshirt – I wore it at the lake. That's it, I swear!"

Marko kept looking at the picture, and I did too. The clothes looked abandoned – left in a heap. There was only one reason why someone would leave their clothes like that at the beach, and not come back for them. So I said it. I asked the obvious question, given Marko wasn't saying anything.

"So do they think it's suicide? That she's left her clothes and walked into the sea?"

Hannah nodded and she looked at Marko as she answered. "Yes. But no one's confirmed anything. Not yet."

And then the news came on the radio.

The body of a young woman was discovered this morning off the shore of Glan y Mor Beach. It was found by a group of fishermen who had chartered a boat for the day from Pwllheli Marina. Glan y Mor Beach is currently closed while police recover the body and begin their investigation. Harlech Beach also remains closed today while police conduct a separate investigation there, thought to be in connection with missing teenager Ceri Rees. Ceri disappeared exactly a week ago today and fears escalate about her safety. A police statement is expected later on this afternoon.

"What the hell?" Hannah said, looking at Marko, her eyes suddenly wider, her voice lower. "Is this seriously happening?"

And then the cafe door swung open and Ifan came flying in.

Hannah stood up.

"Ifan!" she called out, waving at him. "Over here!"

Ifan came straight over and sat down next to Hannah.

"Ifan, I thought you were going to call me," Hannah said, sitting down now too.

"Ifan," Marko said. "You okay?"

"I can't believe she'd do this… I just can't…" Ifan said. His eyes fixed downwards, staring at the table.

Marko and Hannah glanced at each another.

"It doesn't make sense," he said, looking up at Marko. "I'm trying to understand, work it out, but I can't… I don't get it. I just—"

"What do you mean?" Marko asked.

Ifan looked up. "It's Alys, Marko. The body. It has to be."

Hannah reached out to Ifan and he leaned into her, dropping his head on her shoulder. "I'm sorry, Ifan," she said. "I'm just so sorry." And as she said it she looked at Marko and shook her head. She looked pale, in shock. I guessed it was seeing Ifan like that.

"Why did she do it, Hannah?" Ifan said.

I looked across at Marko, but he was looking at Hannah still comforting Ifan. I could see he was struggling to make sense of what Ifan was saying. We all were.

I put my hand on his arm.

"Listen, shall we get some drinks, some food for everyone?"

Marko nodded.

"I'll stay here with Ifan," Hannah said.

I stood up and walked with Marko to the counter, relieved to be away from the table.

Marko was quiet in the queue.

"What are you thinking?" I asked.

"I don't know…"

I nodded. I didn't know what to say.

Hannah was right – I hadn't met Alys. I had no idea what had happened last summer, and while no one was telling me it was hard to even begin to know where to start.

Marko turned to me.

"Alys was just so confident, so sure of herself when we met her. I know we only spent one day with her, but if those are her clothes – if they are – if it's Alys – then I'm finding it hard to understand how it's happened. She just didn't seem to be the sort of person who would do this. I don't know why, but it just doesn't feel right."

"Someone dying, losing someone, it never feels right," I said. "It's a shock too. None of it ever feels right."

"But she was so confident last summer, so her own person," Marko said. "She took us all, a bunch of strangers, out to the lake…I mean if this is a suicide, *her* suicide, then I feel like I'm totally missing something here."

I listened to Marko and thought back to how brave I'd been, going to the beach party when I'd first arrived last Saturday night. It was one of the bravest things I'd ever done, going to a party in a new place with a load of strangers. So what Marko was saying about Alys made some kind of sense. She must have been confident, really confident, to have turned up and hung out with them all like she did. What didn't make sense was why there were all so hung up on her, why she seemed to have had such a huge effect. It seemed they were all still dealing with the fallout from their day with her last summer, even before the news had come today of her death.

"What exactly happened at the lake?" I asked. I lowered my voice as I said it. "None of you seem to be able to explain…"

"If I explain it, I don't think it'll make any sense," Marko said.

"Try me."

"I guess…well, we did stuff with Alys that day that was different. Stuff none of us would normally do. I don't think any of us were our best selves that day, except maybe Ifan. That's what I think when I look back. I don't feel good about that day. I don't think any of us do. But yeah," Marko said. "It's kind of hard to explain."

He stepped forward in the queue. It was driving me

mad the way Marko still didn't seem to want to talk about Alys, or was it that he couldn't?

I looked across at Ifan and Hannah while we waited. They were talking quietly. Ifan seemed calmer.

We were getting closer to ordering the food now. I moved along with Marko in the queue. He was looking at me, like he wanted to say more.

"What is it?" I asked.

"When I went to the hut to get myself set up for my shift yesterday morning, a key had been pushed under the door."

"Okay," I said. "And?"

"I didn't think about it too much when I found it there. I mean, sometimes we do get people handing in stuff that's been left on the beach – lost property…"

"Right."

"But this wasn't a bunch of keys – not like a set of house keys or a car key, no key ring. It was just a single key, a small one, tucked neatly into a folded piece of paper and pushed under the door. Someone had left it there, like that, deliberately."

Marko paused.

"Maybe they found it," I said. "And didn't know how to return it, so they brought it back like that – tucked into a piece of paper they had in their bag or something, so it didn't get lost again, a second time? I can imagine my mum doing something like that."

"You're probably right," Marko said, looking away.

"But what?" I said, trying to pull him back to me, to get him to finish what he'd been trying to say.

"The paper," Marko said, looking at me again now. "It had my name on it."

I looked at him. "Okay…so?"

"I have no idea what this key is for, Cait. Not a clue. It means nothing to me."

He looked like he was almost panicking now.

"So some random key is posted under the door, addressed to me, and I don't know what it's for…and then these clothes are left outside the hut, and Ifan is certain they're Alys's…and now a body's been found up the coast – a young woman's body – and Ifan is telling us it's Alys. This girl Ceri Rees is still missing, and well, I don't know what to think… I'm doubting everything – literally everything – I thought before. Nothing feels normal any more."

I nodded. "What are you saying, Marko?"

"Hannah always said she thought Alys was playing with us last summer, but Hannah didn't like Alys, and I never really believed that was true. But when I think about Alys now, it frightens me. What she did that day, how she behaved, how she made me feel… And I've been beginning to wonder if Hannah and Ifan are right, if Alys's resemblance to the missing girl isn't a ridiculous comparison to make. Because now there are these clothes that look like her clothes and there's this death up the coast and when you put that all together…I don't know… it begins to make me think that this could just be the next move in some sick game Alys has been playing all along, some game we're all involved in now. I know it sounds mad to say it, but right now that's exactly how it feels."

PART
SIX

LAST
SUMMER

MARKO

AT THE LAKE

Hannah didn't move from the rock on the shore. Alys and Ifan swam off and she stayed there, staring into space, looking out across the lake. I followed her gaze. I could see Ifan doing slappy duck. I don't know how many times I'd shown him how to move in the water, how to move with more efficiency and with less splash, and less like a flappy duck, but the guy never learned.

"He looks stupid, doesn't he?" I said, looking at Hannah now. "And you know, I think he really wants to impress her."

"I have no idea why," Hannah said, still staring out at the lake.

I knew Hannah hadn't exactly taken a shine to Alys, but we'd only just met her and I didn't want to ruin the day by getting into some kind of slanging session. Hannah often went in for those. So I changed the subject.

"How are you feeling now?"

Hannah didn't reply. She took a deep breath in, and shivered as she let it out. When she'd first got out of the lake and started having a go at us all, I had wondered if she was in shock. She was really pale and cold. But as soon as we'd got into the car it seemed as if she'd warmed up quite quickly, and that helped.

I squatted down next to her and grabbed her hand. "Are you okay?"

Hannah turned and looked at me and nodded.

I squeezed her hand. "Good," I said. Because I liked Hannah. I really did, and I wanted her to be okay. I knew she could be a pain sometimes, but so could most people I knew. And I'd liked her enough at one point to think that something might happen between us. It had seemed like it was totally possible when I'd been here doing my lifeguard training the summer before last. And when I went back to Birmingham I'd thought about her a lot – we'd messaged each other all the time. But then, when I arrived the following Easter holiday, my heart literally busting at the thought of seeing her and spending time with her, she pretty much dissed me straight off and soon it became clear she was really into this surfer guy who worked at Abersoch. But we stayed friends. So yeah, she can be a right pain – she made me feel a whole load of pain – but as friends go, I wanted to keep her. To be honest I couldn't imagine coming to Wales and staying with Dad and her not being around...so I got over it, got over her, and friends is where we are at.

"It looks like they're coming back," I said to Hannah after we'd sat side by side for a little while in silence. "I'll grab their stuff." I stood up and walked towards the car. I'd left Alys's and Ifan's clothes drying on the bonnet after they'd dropped them on the shingle and swum off.

"Marko?"

"Yeah?" I said, turning back to face Hannah – she was standing up now.

"If there's a spare jumper in the car or a picnic rug, or anything, will you grab it for me?"

I went to answer, but I couldn't, because as Hannah turned away from me to try and sit back down again on the rock, all I could see were the backs of her legs and they were black. Completely black. I could actually see broken veins, the skin mottled and purple where colour was coming through under her skin, spreading like ink in water. She was bruised. Blacks and purples marbled across the back of her thighs. I guessed she must have been like that all over. Her body must have hit the water really hard after she jumped.

"Marko?" she said, waiting for an answer. She was still

standing up, like she was trying to work out how best to sit down again.

"Yeah, sure. I'll see if there's anything in the boot. You still cold then?"

Hannah nodded. "Yeah. I just can't get warm."

She was in shock. She had to be. None of us had seen her jump, seen how she'd landed in the water. She was right to be angry. None of us got it when she'd swum up to the shore and kind of heaved herself onto the beach. We were all too high on our own adrenaline to have noticed.

"Okay," I said, and I went to the car and looked in the boot, but there wasn't anything of any use. We really needed a blanket, a first-aid kit... I opened the rear door and climbed in, lying down on the back seat to look on the floor. Nothing. I peered up and over into the front. There was a sweatshirt. That was something at least. An extra layer. It would do. I leaned forward and grabbed it, and then walked back over to Hannah. I knew I had to get her to put on as many clothes as she could. Most of our stuff was damp or wet from the lake.

"Here," I said. "Put this on."

Hannah reached out for the sweatshirt. "Whose is it?"

"I don't know. It was in the car. It's probably Alys's."

Hannah nodded. "I don't remember her wearing it

earlier," she said and she turned it over in her hands, looking at it, putting it the right way up to get it over her head. "Look, it's filthy. There's a rip on the sleeve."

"It doesn't matter, Hannah. Just put it on. You need to get warm."

Hannah nodded and looked at me, and I saw her eyes fill up with tears. "I just want to go home now, Marko. Can't we just go home?"

"Sure," I said, and I walked over to her. "Come here." I pulled her into me, and I could feel her body shaking against me and I didn't know whether it was the cold or the crying, but I knew holding her like this worked either way. How could I have been so stupid? I was a lifeguard – I was a rescuer, someone who was meant to look out for people, keep them safe. I knew she hadn't wanted to jump into the lake. She'd said she didn't want to. I'd got carried away with Ifan and Alys and I hadn't seen that she was hurt. I'd totally let her down.

Hannah pulled back. "I kind of want to sit down again, but it really hurts."

"Listen, we just need to wait for Ifan and Alys and then we can go. Maybe you can lie down on your side in the car? Do you think that would work?" I said, and as I said it I felt a twinge of Hannah's pain, remembering how battered the back of her body looked. "Just wait there a minute, and I'll call out to Ifan to hurry up and we'll go straight off. I'll make sure we do."

Hannah nodded.

I walked down to the shallows, stepping into the water. Ifan and Alys were still swimming towards us and Ifan was clearly trying to impress. He was swimming ahead of Alys, and just about pulling off a decent stroke… and they were getting closer now.

I waved my arms and beckoned them both in towards us. "Come on!" I shouted. "We need to go!" I watched them continue to swim towards me. I had to be more alert now. I had to be more on it. I glanced back to check on Hannah. She looked okay, for now… I turned back again to the lake…Ifan…all I could see was Ifan…no Alys.

I stepped further into the water. Ifan was still swimming towards us. He didn't seem to have noticed.

"Ifan! Where's Alys?" I shouted.

Ifan turned round to look. He clearly hadn't realized that she'd gone. He'd expected to see her there, still swimming behind him. Had she dived under to spring up on him? To surprise him, as a joke maybe? Perhaps she had…I waited to see.

Ifan was turning round now more quickly, urgently, making more splashes, looking for Alys. It didn't look like this was a joke.

I felt Hannah come up and stand beside me.

"She was behind Ifan a minute ago...she was there, and then she just...went..." Hannah said.

I ran into the water, diving under as soon as it was deep enough. I swam towards Ifan. He was shouting now, shouting to me for help. I didn't have my buoy. I didn't have my colleagues. I didn't have any of the things I would usually have if I'd been in this situation at the beach, but I had to go, because I was trained for this. I'd let Hannah down today. I didn't want to let anyone else down again.

I swam fast, pushing every muscle in my body to get to Ifan.

"It's too murky," he said, as I arrived, his breath raspy. "I can't see anything, and I can't stay under long enough to look..."

I took a deep breath and dived under again trying to calculate how long it had been since we'd last seen Alys. It felt like ages – minutes not seconds – but I knew time behaved strangely in situations like this...maybe it had only been seconds, but anyway, whatever it was, I had to keep looking. If she was under the water then she'd been under too long...

I'd known the water was murky, but Ifan was right – it was almost too murky to see anything at all when you really looked. Even with the light hitting the surface, the water was just full of darkness. And algae. I could see little droplets of the stuff floating around in front of my eyes. It wasn't like the sea at all… I could feel my breath running out now… I needed to take in some air… I rose up to grab some, gasping as I punctured the surface.

Ifan was properly panicking.

"You need to go back," I said. "Be with Hannah. I think she might be in shock."

"But what about Alys?"

"I'll find her," I said. "You go – *now!* And call 999!"

I could see he was tired. Hannah needed someone with her and I didn't need another person to save. He had to go back.

"Just go!" I said.

I watched Ifan turn and start heading towards the shore, and I pulled in another big breath and dived under again, aiming to go deeper this time, as deep as I could. I could hear my heart thumping, the beat of it reminding me of my panic, it was loud in my ears… *I was trained for this*, I said to myself. *I was…* And I swam, pushing down against the water, pushing myself deeper again, but it was getting even harder to see and to swim and then – suddenly – I saw her – swirling in the deep green, bubbles surfacing from her mouth, her nose…was she conscious? I couldn't tell. Was she breathing? She must have been – the bubbles – she *was* breathing…but she looked so calm, too calm…her eyes open…

I kicked out my legs as strongly as I could, feeling my own breath weakening. I had to get to the surface soon, get some air, because there was a pressure building now in my head, a pressure that only some oxygen would relieve…but I had to get to Alys. I had to. I had to bring her with me… I swam towards her and her head turned – she was looking at me – her hair spread around her like a soft fan in the water – something on her wrist glinting – her tiny body somehow floating – she looked like a mermaid…

I grabbed her arm, fast, hard, and I pulled her with me as I kicked and kicked, pushing my way up to the surface, and as I pulled, Alys started to move her arms and her legs in a way she hadn't before, and it helped me, and suddenly we burst through into the air and the light, both of us almost retching as we opened our mouths wide, gasping desperately for air.

I drew Alys towards me, my arms under her shoulders, her back facing me, and I began to swim for the shore. She was so light. I couldn't believe how light she was. It made it easier to swim, but now that I had her, now that I'd heard her take a breath, and then another, my panic eased. And then my body began to ache, to feel weak, to slow, as I swam.

I pushed on, looking at Alys all the time, pushing myself on again towards the shore, and then suddenly she turned her head to look at me. She was so pale, so light, so soft in my arms, and she was smiling now, coughing, then smiling again, but breathing. I could hear her breathing and hearing it helped me with mine, and with the swim, and then I could hear her voice, and she was speaking.

"Sorry," she said. "Were you worried about me?"

I didn't have enough breath to hold her and swim and answer. I blinked my eyes and kind of nodded. All I wanted to do was get her back to the shore now. I needed to focus on getting us both back to the shore.

"You saved me," she said. "We're almost strangers, but you saved me. That's good to know." Then suddenly, without any kind of warning, she wriggled free of my grasp and, as if she'd never been submerged at all, as if what had just happened hadn't happened at all, she began to swim towards the shore, and towards Ifan.

I stopped. I started to tread water, gently, give myself a rest. I watched her swim. She looked almost energized.

"Ifan!" she shouted. "Ifan! Wait for me!"

I carried on watching. I took in the scene – Ifan

smiling, running down to the water's edge to meet Alys, his face full of joy and relief; Alys, her hair leaving an almost golden trail behind her in the water as she swam to meet him; and Hannah on the shore, looking out at me, pale and hurt.

And all I kept thinking was how this morning, when Ifan, Hannah and I had met, ready to spend a day hanging out together at the beach, we'd had no idea of what this day would bring. We didn't know Alys, and we didn't know this place. And even though you can't reverse a decision, or erase a day, I wished in some way that I'd listened to Hannah, that we'd followed her lead like we usually did, and that we'd never ventured out with Alys. How, I wondered, had this strange girl managed to find her way into our lives?

THIS
SUMMER

CAIT

WEDNESDAY

It was cold when I woke up, and I really didn't want to get out of bed. I pulled the cover higher up around my neck, tucking my nose under it and breathing deeply in and out to add to the warmth. I'd got back late last night, later than I should have. I knew Mum wouldn't be happy, but lunch in the cafe had been really intense and we'd ended up all piling back to Ifan's after we'd left. He was really stressed, upset.

Hannah had tried to be nice to him, but I could tell she was still angry somehow, about Alys, and I still didn't get it. Whenever I asked anyone about her they just wouldn't explain. In the end, Marko and I had gone for fish and chips on the beach. It was a relief to get out of Ifan's place. Marko and I huddled together in the wind in front of the dunes and even though I was freezing it felt really nice, just being there with him, and blocking the rest of the world out. I ignored a whole load of Mum's texts while

I was out. I knew that was wrong and that she was going to be mad at me, but I just didn't want to go home and sit and watch TV with her and Johnny like some kind of third wheel. Lucky for me she'd been in bed when I'd got in.

I took another deep breath, and braced myself to get out of bed and face the cold, and Mum's inevitable rant, when I heard voices. It sounded like Mum and Johnny were arguing. I'd never heard them argue before. I guessed it was possibly about me, which suddenly made me feel bad. Was I ruining this holiday for Mum? I didn't want to mess things up for her, not really, but it was all just so weird here with Johnny. And now with these new friends freaking out, being upset, this missing girl... As soon as Mum had mentioned us all coming away together I'd known the holiday would be weird, but it was turning out to be even weirder than I could ever have imagined.

I slid under the duvet with my phone. There was a message from Mia.

Hey. How was the beach party? You never replied... Any hot surfer types? Do you even get those in Wales?

I messaged back.

If a lifeguard counts – yes, you do…

I smiled. Thank god for my phone. Thank god for Mia. Thank god for Marko, who seemed to provide a little splash of light in this seriously muddy puddle.

I looked at my phone again. I wanted to hear from Marko, but it was early and, well, there probably wasn't really anything to say. It didn't feel right to just text some kind of hi or hello or some little message about nothing in particular after everything that had happened yesterday.

I heard the front door slam shut.

I sat up. I guessed Johnny had gone out. I put my phone on the side, stuffed my feet into my slippers and went downstairs.

Mum was sitting at the kitchen table, staring into her mug of tea. She looked up when I came in. She looked tired.

"You okay?" I said.

Mum nodded.

"Johnny gone to get the paper?" I asked, sitting down.

"Yes," Mum said. "Listen, I want to talk to you. I didn't like the way you just left yesterday. You went out and you didn't tell me where you were going and I didn't hear from you for the rest of the day. You can't do that. Especially what with this missing girl, and now the body they've found. I thought it would be safer here than in London, but it turns out that that might not be the case, and so actually the same rules need to apply here as they do at home. I need to know where you're going and who you're going with. I need to know where you are."

"Great place we've come on holiday to, eh, Mum?" I said, trying to lighten the mood, but she didn't pick up and run with it like she normally would. She just kept staring into her tea.

"So what are they saying about the body? Is there any more news?" I asked, trying to change the subject.

"No," Mum said. "I've not heard anything." She looked up at me. "Aren't you going to say anything? Say sorry about yesterday, going off like you did? You seem more interested in this body, this missing girl, than what's going on with us!"

"I just forgot to say where I was going, that's all. I told you I was going out. I'm sure I did."

"You didn't!" Mum said. "And you didn't reply to any of my messages or texts!"

"Well I'm sorry then!" I said. "I thought I did!" But I knew that I didn't sound sorry, and that was because I wasn't, and Mum knew that too. "And anyway, what's so wrong with being interested in what's happened to Ceri Rees?"

"I didn't say there was anything wrong with it," Mum said.

"She's almost the same age as me."

"I know!" Mum said. "And that's why I was so worried yesterday, that's why I didn't like how you went off like you did! That's why I needed you to text me back or call me!"

"Did you know she lost her mum and her stepsister in a car accident two years ago?" I said. I could hear anger in my voice, but I wasn't sure why it was there. "She's been living with her stepdad ever since. She has no one!"

Mum looked at me.

"I'm not sure what you're trying to say, Cait."

"I'm not trying to say anything!" I said, but my voice was loud again. Too loud.

"I'm not planning on eloping with Johnny any time soon, if that's what you're worried about!" Mum was shouting now. "And I'm not planning on dying or disappearing on you either! For god's sake, Cait!"

I stood up. I couldn't believe how Mum was only seeing things from her own point of view. She never used to be like this. Why couldn't she see how it was for me? Was it so wrong to be feeling like I did? I mean couldn't she see – couldn't she understand – once you've lost one parent you just can't afford to lose another. All this holiday seemed to have done was make Mum feel further away from me, like she was slipping further away all the time.

"I didn't think you were planning to run off and marry Johnny any time soon!" I said, shouting back. "That's not what I'm saying!" I wanted to scream. I wanted to scream so loud that the whole freezing cold stupid little cottage collapsed around us! But I didn't. Instead I walked towards the door to leave the room, turning back to Mum before I did. "And by the way, I'm going out! I'm getting dressed and going out and you don't need to worry about me! I'll be okay!" I slammed the door. Hard. Again. All I seemed to have done these last few days was leave, slamming doors.

2

I got dressed and slipped out of the house quietly before Johnny got back. I'd heard Mum come upstairs and go into the bathroom. I'd wondered if she might come in and try and make things better, sort things out, but she didn't. So I went out into the garden, through the gate and onto the estuary. It was peaceful here, and walking among the grasses and reeds, following the little winding channels, the trickling streams, it seemed to create a little bit of space in my heart.

I walked out onto the sands – the tide looked like it might have been turning – I couldn't see which way the water was flowing. I stopped and watched for a bit to see if I could work it out, and then I turned to look back at the cottages. I wondered if Marko was in, if he or his dad would have heard Mum and me fighting. The cottages were close together. I guessed it was possible that they could have heard some of the shouting.

And then I saw a figure…Marko, I was pretty sure it was him – walking out onto the estuary towards me. I smiled. I couldn't help myself. I guessed if he had heard what had just happened with Mum, and I explained, he'd understand…but even though I stood by how I felt, I suddenly didn't feel that good about how I'd just been with Mum. I didn't really want to fight with her like this.

I stood and waited for Marko.

"I saw you coming out. I thought I'd say hi."

"Hi," I said, smiling again.

We walked together a little way alongside the main channel of water, which was now snaking its way out towards the horizon and the sea. The tide was going out. I was pretty sure of that now.

"I've just had a fight with my mum," I said. "We seem to have had a few since we've been here." I looked up at him to see if he might have known, heard.

Marko nodded. "Yeah, parents. Not easy, eh?"

If he'd heard, he wasn't going to say.

"You get on with yours okay?"

"Yes. I mean it's much easier being here with Dad. He just lets me get on with my own thing. He treats me like a grown-up. With my mum, it's different. She's on at me all the time. That's kind of why I come here. I need the break. And of course it's nice to see Dad, but you know, he can be pretty, well…removed. He's at his desk a lot."

I thought about Dad. He hadn't been at all removed from me or Mum when he was alive. It always felt like he was present. Maybe I'd taken that for granted. Maybe that's why it felt so hard with him gone.

"What was your dad like?" Marko asked.

"Oh, I was just thinking about that – you know, he was great. Really great." I didn't feel I could say any more without getting upset, and I didn't want to get upset now.

Marko nodded. "You miss him?"

"Yeah," I said.

"Stupid question," Marko said. "Of course you do."

"This is our first holiday without him," I said. "It's still hard getting used to him not being here. And, you know, Johnny is here. That's kind of hard too."

"Johnny?"

"Yeah, Mum's new boyfriend, partner, whatever. I'm not sure what I should call him."

"Oh right. Yeah, that must be hard."

"It is," I said. "And then Mum and me fighting a lot. Some holiday!"

Marko turned to me and we stopped walking. He pulled me in towards him, wrapping his arms around me, and for a moment I felt totally safe. I hadn't known how much I'd needed that hug, but I had.

I pulled back, my arms now holding Marko's, his holding mine. We looked at each other.

"Thanks," I said. "That was nice."

"I like you, Cait," Marko said. "I really like you."

I nodded and smiled. "I like you too," I said, but the joy I knew I should be feeling right now wasn't there, because all I could think about was how this holiday, this nice thing with Marko, whatever it was, was going to have to end. Just like everything else. I hated that when things went right, the first thought I'd have was that.

Marko's phone suddenly rang.

"I think I better get it," he said, "I'm sorry." He pulled his phone out of his pocket.

"Sure," I said, as Marko swiped to answer.

"Ifan? You okay?"

Silence.

"Sure. I can come now," Marko said, and he hung up.

"What's going on?"

I could see by Marko's face that something had happened. His mood had changed.

"Ifan wants us to go to the hut, now – me and Hannah. He said he'll meet us there."

I nodded. "Right. I'll walk back to the cottages with you then."

"You should come too," Marko said.

"Really? I mean, what about Hannah?"

"What about her?" Marko said.

"She's not my biggest fan, or hadn't you noticed?"

"Forget about Hannah. Honestly. You shouldn't worry about her or what she thinks of you."

I nodded. "So there's nothing going on between you both? No history? You're not together?"

"No!" Marko said. "No – we're friends. Just friends. I promise. Come on, we should start walking back. Ifan said to get over there as soon as I could." He reached over and took my hand, and he looked at me as we started to walk. "I want you to come with me," he said and he squeezed my hand tight. "I really do."

When we got to the hut Ifan and Hannah were already there. Ifan was pacing up and down. The hut was small, but he still somehow seemed to be covering a lot of ground; his steps were short, almost manic. Hannah was leaning against the locker, arms crossed, watching him. She didn't look happy at all.

"Your mate Luke is on duty," Ifan said to Marko. "I asked him and he said we could use the hut. We've got about half an hour."

"What's going on?" Marko said.

"Well, I've been waiting for you to get here so we can find out!" Hannah said. She ignored me. Just like she always did. I wasn't quite sure where to put myself in the room.

Ifan stopped walking and looked up at us all.

"I went to the police this morning. I made a formal statement."

"Good," Hannah said. "I'm glad. What made you change your mind?"

"Finding the clothes on the beach," Ifan said. "The police asked me a few questions yesterday. I told them that I knew who the clothes belonged to. They invited me to the station to make a formal statement after that. So I went this morning and I told them about Alys. I told them everything."

"What do you mean everything?" Marko said.

Ifan was calm. Almost too calm. I could see that it was making Marko nervous. For some reason I felt nervous now too.

"I mean I told them about meeting Alys last summer, the day at the lake, how I haven't been able to get hold of her since. I told them she looks like the missing girl."

"And? What did they say?" Hannah asked.

"I think they're just humouring me," Ifan said. "They told me that they don't have any missing persons on their register by the name of Alys, and of course we don't know her surname. So it's kind of my word, my story, my recognition of her in this photo – and in terms of something for the police to work on, well…it's nothing. And it's not like I could say that I've seen her any time recently. They think I'm in love, lovesick. They kind of laughed at me – laughed in my face."

"Lovesick. They got that right!" Hannah said quickly – too quickly – and then she carried on to try and cover up her sharp tongue. "But weren't they interested in anything you were telling them?"

Ifan shook his head. He looked crushed. He wasn't calm. He was numb. Like the shock of Alys's death had stretched out its long fingers and grasped him, stifling all the feelings he had raging inside. I recognized that grasp. I'd lived with it, fought with it. I could still feel it sometimes, even now.

Everyone was quiet for a moment.

"I'm sorry, Ifan," I said, "I'm really sorry," because I could see the pain, like a scribble across his face.

"But what about the clothes?" Marko said. He looked serious now.

"They've bagged them up, taken them away. Apparently they need someone to identify them as Ceri's. But honestly, it's a waste of time."

"So the police think they're Ceri's clothes?" I said, looking at Ifan again.

"Yes, they're acting like they are. But they aren't the clothes Ceri was last seen in, according to the poster and the reports. And I swear to god, they're Alys's. They're the exact clothes Alys was wearing last summer."

"I agree they look just like them, Ifan," Hannah said,

"but I guess the police have to check everything out. Technically the clothes could be anybody's until they do."

I could tell Hannah was trying to make things better for Ifan, somehow soften things, maybe even create some hope that this wasn't Alys, but she really wasn't getting it right.

"They're *her* clothes, Hannah, *her* things!" Ifan said, his voice suddenly louder. "No one else has shoes with those drawings and doodles all over them. The shoes were there, with the clothes, and her bracelet too, with the leaf. She's dead, Hannah!" And then he shook his head, and I could see that he wanted to cry but he couldn't get the tears out. "She's dead and everyone is thinking about Ceri, not Alys, and no one is listening to me!"

It felt really awkward suddenly – *I* felt really awkward – like I shouldn't have been there. But I wanted to say something. So I did.

"Is it not possible that Ceri lied and called herself Alys the day she met you all?"

Ifan shot me a look. Anger.

"I've thought about that too," Hannah said. "I didn't want to say it, because I know you don't want to hear it or think it, but…"

I stepped in to save Hannah. I'm not sure why I did,

but she was flailing around with her words, still trying to find the right thing to say, and not getting there fast enough, and Ifan was just breaking apart in front of us now.

"I know it doesn't make things any better," I said, looking at Ifan. "It doesn't change what's happened today – the clothes, this death. But it's possible, isn't it?"

"I didn't trust her," Hannah went on. "I always said to you that I thought she was playing with us." She looked at Marko to agree, but he didn't say anything.

I just wanted Hannah to shut up now.

"Alys didn't lie to me! I'm sure of that!" Ifan said.

I noticed Hannah and Marko share a look again. A look I'd seen them share before.

"You didn't like her, Hannah. And that's okay," Ifan went on. "But I *did* like her. I trusted her. And she trusted me too. That's the worst thing about all this. She trusted me. And when it came to it this summer, I let her down because I didn't know what to do."

There was silence for a moment.

"Did the police say anything to you about the body at Glan y Mor?" Marko asked.

"They wouldn't tell me anything," Ifan said. "But I know – I just know it's her."

Ifan stopped and looked away from us all. He pressed

his lips together and folded his arms tightly across his chest. He took a deep breath in, and started pacing again. It looked like he was having a fight with himself – an internal battle – the words trying to make their way out, his body trying to suck them back in.

"For god's sake, Ifan!" Hannah said. "What's going on? Just tell us! I know I didn't like Alys, but we're all suffering here with you, thinking about last summer, how it was that day—"

"She was a good swimmer," Marko said, interrupting. "I went to rescue her in the lake, I thought she was drowning, but you know, she was okay…and I never really understood that. She told me that I saved her that day. But I never really felt like I did…and now what? She's drowned? She's actually drowned?"

It sounded like Marko was going back over the day in his head. That was the first I'd heard about Alys nearly drowning. Why hadn't he said anything about it before?

"What happened when you swam off with her at the lake?" Hannah asked. "I swear something happened, Ifan. Why won't you say?"

So there was stuff that happened that day that they'd kept from each other, still now? I was desperate – as desperate as they were – to know it all.

Ifan spoke. He was calmer now.

"Alys showed me a tattoo. A tiny blue butterfly tattoo. It was on her hip. She said that no one else knew about it but me."

"And?" Hannah said. "So what?" She was annoyed again, but I could see that underneath it all she was frightened too.

"She asked me to keep it a secret. I didn't understand. I asked her if she was okay. She said she was... I didn't think she'd do this – kill herself...if I'd known she'd meant this, I'd have never—"

"But you couldn't have known," I said. "How could you?"

"I said I'd keep her secret," Ifan went on, "because that's what she wanted me to do. But today I told the police. I told them about the tattoo, and what she'd said. I don't know if I've done the right thing. Alys said she trusted me to know when to do the right thing, but I don't – I didn't – and now I just feel like I've let her down. Betrayed her trust in me...and now she's dead."

Ifan looked broken.

"You did the right thing," I said. "Because the tattoo will identify her. The police will know one way or the other if that body at Glan y Mor is hers, because of that."

Silence.

I felt sick. Talking about this body – it wasn't just a body

– it was someone. It was a life, and it was gone.

Hannah spoke – "And you definitely saw it, Ifan? This tattoo? It definitely exists?"

Ifan nodded. And then he bent down and picked up a grey metal lock-box and put it onto the desk. "Yesterday I found this. It was by the bins at the back of the Coffee Shack. It must have been left over the weekend. I literally tripped over it. It wasn't there when I put the rubbish out on Friday."

I looked at Marko. I thought about the key, posted under the hut door. Could it have been a key to a lock-box like this?

Marko stepped forward.

"It's locked," Ifan said. "I've tried to get it open, but I can't."

"So?" Hannah said. "What is it?"

I looked at Marko again, and I looked at the box, willing him to say something before I did.

"I know you don't want to hear it, Ifan," Hannah said. "I know you think Alys liked you, and trusted you, but she lied. She did. She was a liar."

"What do you mean?" Ifan said.

Hannah went on.

"I went to see her. Last summer. After the day at the lake."

"Just leave it, Hannah, will you?" Marko said, stepping forward now, towards the box. "Let's get this open, find out what's in it."

"What? You saw her and you never told me?" Ifan said looking at Hannah, ignoring Marko now.

He was angry again.

"Do you know how freaked out I was after that day?" Hannah said. "Neither of you waited for me on the cliff. I was stressed out and frightened, and neither of you even gave me a second thought. You left me. And I was hurt after I jumped. I was aching, sore, covered in bruises, and I was freaked out by Alys and how she'd kind of, well, taken us over, taken us all in – you especially, Ifan. It was like she had some kind of hold over you."

"I liked her! Surely you could see that's what it was, Hannah! It wasn't going to stop you and me being friends!"

"Except you weren't my friend that day, Ifan! You weren't!" Hannah shouted.

Ifan was shouting now too.

"I can't believe you went to see Alys and you never told me – how could you do that when you knew how much I wanted to see her?"

Hannah didn't answer.

"Ifan, Hannah," Marko said, looking at them both,

trying to calm things down. "There's no point in going over all this stuff. It's not going to help."

Ifan turned to Marko. "You don't know that! How do you know that?"

Marko was quiet. I could see he was lost; he didn't know what to do.

Ifan turned back to Hannah. "So did you find her?" he said. "Did you find Alys when you went to look for her?"

Hannah nodded.

"When?" Ifan said, stepping towards Hannah.

"About a week later, a week after our day at the lake, maybe longer, I don't exactly remember when."

Ifan was hanging off Hannah's every word. Every bit of him was on alert, waiting to hear what she was going to say next.

"I went to the caravan park, where she said she was staying. I walked all around, asked around, and I was just about to give up looking when I saw her. She was by the entrance, looking through the bins. She looked really dirty. That skanky sweatshirt of hers I borrowed was even dirtier than it had been before."

"Did you know about this?" Ifan said, looking at Marko.

"Yes," Marko said. He looked embarrassed, ashamed.

"And you didn't think to tell me?"

"I wanted to tell you, I really did, but you were hurting enough, and I thought it was best for you not to know what Hannah had found—"

"She seemed really different," Hannah said, carrying on now. "She said she was looking for something she'd lost, like she was explaining why she was going through the bins. She was kind of flustered, less confident. I swear she was looking for food. I felt like I'd caught her out in some way. I know that sounds strange..."

"Go on," Ifan said.

"I suggested we get a cup of tea or a drink or something," Hannah said. "The caravan park had a cafe and a little playground, a shop. I said I'd get some food, something that we could eat in her caravan. I said that I'd love to meet her little brother, her sister. I just wanted to talk to her, find out who she was, what she was doing spending that day with us like she had, doing what she did, and then disappearing and not calling you. I was trying to be a friend, Ifan. I was trying to work her out, find her out, but I was also trying to be a friend – to *you*."

"So what did she say?" Ifan asked.

"She said she had stuff she needed to do. She didn't really look at me. Not properly. She just wanted to get away. I could tell. I told her you'd been trying to get hold of her. I asked her if she'd lost her phone – I said that you'd been trying her, Ifan, and getting a dead tone, and that you really wanted to see her again."

"She gave me her number," Ifan said. "She told me to call her. She wouldn't have done that unless she liked me. Don't you remember how she was with me? How we were on the journey home? She liked me. She did."

Ifan looked from Hannah to Marko for a response.

"I just remember how quiet it was in the car after we left the lake," Marko said. "That's all."

Hannah nodded. "Me too."

"Once I got out of the water you called the ambulance off," Marko said. "Hannah was tearful. She just wanted to get back home. We packed up quickly at the lakeshore and we left. It felt to me like none of us had anything to say to each other after that."

"Alys and I did," Ifan said. "She told me she wanted to see me again. She gave me her number. We kissed."

Hannah looked at Ifan. "This is why I didn't tell you, why Marko didn't either. I really didn't want to tell you this—"

"Just tell me, Hannah!" Ifan said.

"She said she didn't want to see you, that she'd given you some made-up number. She said it was one day, and it was just a bit of fun – a distraction from other stuff she had going on – and it didn't mean anything, and—"

"I don't believe she said that," Ifan said.

"I told Marko about seeing her because I had to tell someone and I didn't know what else to do. I didn't want to hurt you, Ifan. It seemed pretty clear to me she was playing with us all, but whenever I said that to you, you wouldn't listen. And I wished I was wrong about her, but when I found her, it just confirmed that I was right. Nothing she told us hung together. There was no little brother, no sister, no family at all as far as I could see. She was alone. And she just seemed to have spat all over you and your feelings with whatever it was she said to you at the lake."

"That's not true," Ifan said. "It's not." He started pacing again.

"I'm sorry, Ifan," Hannah said. "But maybe now you can see why I've been so down on her. I think all this – the clothes on the sand outside the hut, this lock-box or whatever that is –" Hannah said gesturing to the box on the desk – "if it *is* her, then it's games, isn't it? She's playing with you again, with all of us, except now she's dead, and we don't know why or what she did this for, and we're left with it. *All* of us. And I know you hate me for not telling you any of this before now, but you're my friend and I did it for the right reasons, because I don't want to see you hurt like this – I—"

"There's something else," Marko said, interrupting.

He looked at me and then he walked over to his locker and pulled out a folded piece of paper with his name handwritten across it. He put it down on the desk, and opened it up. And there, sitting on the white open page, between the folds, was the key.

"I don't know if this is something or nothing, but I found it here when I came in for my shift first thing yesterday. Someone had pushed it under the hut door, like this, addressed to me."

Ifan looked at the lock-box, and then back at Marko and the key.

It was quiet. Suddenly so quiet after all the words that had been shouted and shared.

I could sense that Marko and Hannah were waiting for Ifan to say something, to tell them what they should do.

"So try it," Ifan said to Marko. It almost sounded like a challenge the way he said it. I could see the fury in his face.

"No," Marko said. "You found the box. You do it." And he held out the key to Ifan.

Ifan didn't move.

"Come on, Ifan!" Hannah said.

Ifan shook his head. "I can't do it. I don't want to.

The key was addressed to you, Marko. You do it."

Marko pulled the lock-box towards him. He stuck the key in the lock and turned. There was a neat click.

My tummy flipped.

I felt sick. I wanted to know what was inside, but I was almost too scared to look.

"It worked," Marko said. "It's open."

We all moved closer together to stand over it.

"You open it," Hannah said to Ifan.

I watched as Ifan lifted it. I could see there were a few objects inside. I was desperate to see them, but I knew I couldn't be as desperate as the others were.

Ifan put his hand into the box. He pulled something out. I couldn't work out what it was at first, but then I recognized it; a white plastic tag from a hospital, just like the one Mum had kept from when I was born. Ifan held it up. There was a blue biro scrawl on the tag, which read *Baby Ceri Rees* and alongside, *Mother's Name:* – the scrawl again – *Maddie Rees*. Ifan passed the tag on to Marko, and pulled out the next thing – a wedding ring and an engagement ring, all sparkly stones and scratched dull gold, like they'd seen better days. Hannah reached out for them and Ifan put them in her open palm. And then he lifted out a driving licence, and he read the name on it. "Maddie Rees-Roberts," he said, and he passed it over for me to hold and I looked at the photograph. An older woman with pale brown shoulder-length hair and such soft eyes, staring back at me from the picture…and then a bank card, now on the desk, the name on it, *Ceri Rees*. And last of all, a small postcard with an illustration of a tiny blue butterfly on the front. Ifan held it for a couple of minutes and then passed it around for us all to see – and the handwritten words on the other side said: *For my darling daughter, my butterfly blue, I will always and forever love you. xx*

No one spoke. Each of us held an item, and looked at it.

"These are Ceri's things," I said. "They belong to Ceri Rees."

I looked around the group. There was silence. I could feel their confusion, their shock. I felt it too.

"I think we have to go to the police," I said.

And then I looked over and into the bottom of the lock-box, to see if there was anything else…

"There's still this," I said, lifting it out. "It looks like a letter."

I held it up. It didn't seem to be addressed to anyone. I could see the handwriting through the folds. I went to pass it to Marko, but he shook his head and wouldn't take it.

"Cait's right," Marko said. "We need to go to the police."

"But what about this?" I said, pushing the letter closer to Ifan. "Don't you want to read it? Don't you think we *need* to?"

I couldn't believe they were all standing there so quietly, not saying anything. I wanted to know what was in the letter. Why didn't they want to know too?

"I don't think we should look at the letter," Marko said. He seemed scared. "We need to hand everything over to the police. It's evidence," he said. "I'm guessing it's a note, a suicide note. It's not for us."

"But it was left *here*, wasn't it?" Hannah said. "It has to have been left for us. She's left all this *here* – for *us*! Can't you see?"

I looked at Ifan. He was standing completely still, staring at a point on the floor. He wasn't saying anything, and it frightened me now that he wasn't and that no one else seemed to have noticed.

"But we don't actually know who put the box here, or what it means," said Marko and he shifted on his feet and pulled his hands through his hair. He was panicking, but trying to hide it. "This is Ceri Rees's stuff. She's missing. It's evidence. The police will know what to do. It's for them to sort out, not us."

"And the postcard?" I said. "With the butterfly blue?" I looked at Ifan. I wanted him to say something, do something. Why wasn't he saying anything? Surely the blue butterfly tattoo he'd described wasn't just some mad coincidence here?

"I don't like this," Hannah said, cutting across me, still ignoring Ifan. "I'm scared. How are we going to even begin to explain all this to the police? We can't!"

Marko walked over to Hannah and put his hand on her arm. "Hannah, listen. The police will know what to do."

Suddenly Ifan spoke.

"We need to read the letter," he said, his voice calm, controlled.

"What?" Marko said, turning quickly to face him.

"It's the right thing to do," Ifan said. "I know it is. Trust me."

Hannah and Marko looked at one another, and then back at Ifan.

I went to pass the letter over to Ifan, but he didn't move.

"I'm not reading it out," he said, looking at Marko and Hannah. "It has to be one of you."

"Well I'm not doing it!" Hannah said. "I'm not reading it out. No way. Not me."

"Marko?" Ifan said. "You do it."

Marko shook his head. "I told you, I don't think we should read it. I vote we go to the police. If you think we should read it, Ifan, then why don't you?"

"You both seem to think you know Alys better than me," Ifan said. "And maybe you do." He paused for a moment. He looked so hurt. "I want to know what's in the letter, but I can't read it out right now. You think you know her? You read the letter."

I could see the sadness around Ifan. He was wearing it like a cloak. I wanted to go to him, help him, but I knew I couldn't do that. I couldn't make it better for him. No one could. But there was one thing I could do.

"I'll read the letter," I said. "I'll do it. If you'd like me to."

Hannah, Marko and Ifan all looked at me.

"Go on then," Hannah said. "You read it out. You be the one."

And so, even though I felt sick with how much I was feeling for Ifan, I opened the letter and began to read.

THIS SUMMER

ALYS

Dear Ifan, Marko and Hannah

When I first saw you all sitting, talking, laughing by the lifeguard hut on the beach, you all looked so happy. It was kind of intoxicating. I watched you for a little while, and then I kept on watching. I couldn't stop. All I wanted was to have what you all had. And as I watched I only had one thought – I want to be a part of that. The day we spent together at the lake was one of the best. If I hadn't seen you that day, spent it with you, I'm not sure I would have ever done what I did. So I want to say thank you. And I hope that if you feel what I have done is wrong, you will find a way to forgive me, and if you don't understand why I am doing what I'm doing now, this letter will in some way help you try.

Two years ago, I lost my mum and my stepsister, Mariam, in a car crash. Mum was driving and the car swerved off the road. We hit a post. I don't remember what happened after that, except that Mum and Mariam died and I was the one who, against all the odds, survived. And since the crash all I've done is try and work out why I was the one who was left. Sometimes I hate my mum for dying, for leaving me like she did, and then I hate myself for hating her like this. And then I look at my stepdad and all I can see is my own disappointment staring back at me, doubled, tripled, with his own pain – because I don't want him, and he doesn't want me. I want my mum and Mariam, and he wants them too. Being at home without them is suffocating – we don't know how to be, or what to do – and every day it feels like we are wading through the thickest murk, and I know what that is – it's loss – it's guilt – and neither of us are making it through.

So I run away. It's what I do to cope with things. I head to the caravan park in Llanbedr because I can find food there, use the toilets, sleep in the woods on the edge of the park, hang out and pretend I'm somebody else. I do it for a day or two and then I go back home, and try again with my stepdad. Going away like that gives me the space to breathe. It helps. And I thought I could keep doing that for the next year – escaping for a bit and coming back – until I was eighteen and could talk to my stepdad, explain to him why I needed to go, and leave home for good. You see, he thinks he needs to hold on to me – look after me, for Mum. We'd been a family – him and Mariam, Mum and me – for just two years before they died. My dad left when I was born. Without my stepdad, I have no one. He knows this. And he is trying.

But last week, we had an argument. He screamed, I wish you were dead and I screamed back, I wish you were dead too, and then I knew. It was clear. I couldn't wait any longer, live like this. I had to go.

Ifan, when I showed you my tattoo, I showed you the most precious thing in the world to me – something that was home, that was Mum, that will forever be a part of me – and somehow doing that made me free. I know I wasn't clear when we talked in the cave, but I want you to know that in some strange and unexpected way I opened my heart to you that day and I'm so glad that I did.

So I'm writing this letter as I hide out in the dunes at Harlech Beach. This is my second night here. I came from the campsite a couple of days ago. I had planned to come and find you all, but when I saw a missing poster with my name and picture pinned to a telegraph pole on the main road out of the campsite, I panicked. I knew I couldn't stay in the area any longer unless I wanted to be found. So I turned back and walked along the coast path, away from the road, and I worked out pretty quickly, as I walked, that I needed to dump all the stuff I had with me. If anyone saw me, or my stuff, they'd know exactly who I was. And I don't want to be found, taken home, back to the sadness, the loss, the murk because that's where the monsters lie now. And the truth is I don't want to be Ceri any more. I want to be the girl who hung out with you all last summer – the loud and fearless girl who was free enough to shriek and jump and swim. I want to be her. I want to be Alys.

Hannah, Marko – I owe you an apology. I'm sorry if I frightened you. I know that I did. Ifan – I let you down. You have to know that what I said to Hannah when she came to the caravan park after our day at the lake wasn't how I felt about you. I lied because I'd been caught out, and I'm sorry. I lied to you all about a few things – about being here on holiday, about my family, about my age – because I had to – because I'd run away – because I didn't want to be who I was – because it felt better for me to pretend I was someone else.

So I'm going to put this letter in the lock-box and I'll tuck it by the bins behind the Coffee Shack. I'm leaving it for you to find, Ifan. The box will be locked, but I will push the key under the hut door. I think that's the safest thing to do. I know it's a massive gamble that you'll find the box, Ifan – and Marko, that you'll find the key – but each of you, in your own way, saved me last summer, and I guess if you are reading this now, as I hope you are, then my gamble will have paid off.

I haven't quite decided where I'll go now, but I know that when I go I will leave my clothes, the dirtiest ones, the skanky ones I don't want or need any more, in a pile on the sand, so it looks like I've gone – totally gone – like I've walked myself through the waves and way out into the sea. It will break my heart to do this – I know my mum wouldn't like it – but this is what I need to do. Maybe tonight. Maybe tomorrow. Definitely soon.

So when you read this, if you do, I'll be gone, but in going I have just one thing left to ask, one last request, if you like, before I go – and that's to keep me, my things, my secret safe. So I can go. Be free. Be brave like Alys. And I promise I will come back to you, when I can.

xx

PART
NINE

THIS
SUMMER

CAIT

THURSDAY

"Morning," Mum said, glancing up from her paper as I walked into the kitchen. The radio was on – some gentle classical musical – not Johnny's mad rock rubbish like before.

"Hi," I said.

I wasn't really sure how to be with Mum. Our goodbye yesterday was basically me slamming a door in her face for the second time, and then I'd come in late from the beach again too, because I'd stayed on at the hut to be with everyone.

I'd read Ceri's letter again, two, maybe three times. The others were arguing about the box and what to do with the stuff. Ifan was reeling between sadness and confusion, and still wanted to know about the body on the beach. He just couldn't let go of the possibility that it could still be Alys. It didn't seem to matter to him that the letter made it clear that Ceri had lied about being Alys, that she'd left us her things – her Ceri things – that she'd run away. He just couldn't quite take it all in.

And I understood why Ifan felt like he did, why he couldn't quite see Ceri in all of this. Because the girl he knew *was* Alys – to him she would always be Alys. It didn't matter about the box or the letter. As far as he was concerned, until he knew whose body had been found, Alys could still be dead.

But I was sure, after I'd read the letter for a third time, that Ceri was alive – that she'd faked her death and run. She'd just gone further away this time, made a more permanent plan. And I understood why she'd done that. I knew that feeling of wanting to get away from yourself, to be free from all you think and feel, because some days it's too hard and you just want to be somebody else. I think maybe I understood it in a way that the others didn't, because of losing Dad.

Marko tried to persuade us all to go to the police, and Hannah was just still so angry that she couldn't think around any of it. Nothing was going to take that anger away from her. Everyone was stuck not knowing what to do, and eventually Marko and I walked out and got some chips and drinks from a van on the main road, to break it all up, create some space. And when we got back to the beach we sat down and we kept on talking until none of us could really talk any more. They explained everything that had happened at the lake, and once they'd finished telling me we sat quietly together, shocked and exhausted from the day, and from still wanting to know whether the body was Ceri or not. The possibility nagged at us all.

As the light began to fade, Ifan stood up, clutching the lock-box and the letter – he'd brought it with him, had it at his feet while we'd talked. *I'm going to take these home*, he said. *For tonight. Keep them safe, for Alys.* And the rest of us just nodded, even Marko didn't try and stop him, and then we all headed home.

"You okay?" I said, looking over at Mum now, and slowly slicing some bread and putting it in the toaster. I was so tired after yesterday, and I was waiting for her to start giving me a lecture, start having a go. The thought of having to defend myself somehow, even though I knew I was in the wrong, was making me tired too.

"I'm fine," she said.

She carried on reading.

I listened to the mechanical tick of the timer on the toaster, and waited for her to say something more, but she didn't.

And then it struck me that I hadn't heard Johnny this morning. I usually heard him clearing his throat in the bathroom, going down the stairs, annoyingly humming his way around the house and creeping back up again with Mum's cup of tea.

"Where's Johnny?" I asked. As Mum already had the newspaper, I guessed he must have gone off on his own for a walk or something. Probably so she could tear me apart.

"He's gone home," she said. She didn't look up.

"Oh," I said. "Oh, right."

Had something happened between them? I couldn't quite believe that he'd just left. Had they argued again? Not made up? Was it because of me?

"He went about an hour ago. He's gone back to London on the train. He decided to head home early," she said.

There was silence.

I wasn't sure what to say. I knew Mum liked Johnny. She'd said she loved him. I didn't want her to be sad. Not that she looked all that sad. She actually looked quite happy, at peace, sitting here with her newspaper and the music on. I wondered what had happened. I was glad that he'd gone, but I felt kind of bad if he'd gone because of me.

"Are you okay?" I said. "I mean, him going home early—"

"It's fine," Mum said, looking up at me at last. "The holiday, him being here, it wasn't really working."

The toast leaped out of the toaster, making me jump.

I grabbed it, quickly, and dropped it down in front of me on a plate before heading to sit at the table with Mum.

I looked at her as I sat and tried a smile, but it didn't come out right, because I didn't know if she was still angry from yesterday, or maybe angry because she blamed me for Johnny leaving – or both.

She looked across at me.

"I think you and I need a bit of time, just the two of us. What do you think?"

I nodded and a smile, this time a natural one, a normal one, broke across my face without me even having to think about it. Like a rising sun, I could almost feel its warmth on my face. I was so glad to hear her say that.

She reached across the table and grabbed my hand and squeezed it, and I squeezed hers back.

"But what about you and Johnny?" I asked. "Are you okay? Like *really* okay? You aren't splitting up or anything?"

"Look," Mum said, "I love Johnny. I love him a lot, and I'm going to keep seeing him. Who knows what will happen or where it will go from here."

I nodded. I didn't like hearing her say that she loved him, but I guessed she was being honest. If she was being honest then I could be too.

"You know, I do think he's a keeper," Mum said. "So I am going to try and make it work."

I cringed. I really didn't want to hear Mum talking like that about a man who wasn't my dad. It was just wrong, plain wrong, to hear it. If Dad was still here this conversation wouldn't even be happening; I wouldn't even have to be a part of it. But he wasn't. And remembering that just made me feel so sad again.

"But I think coming together on this holiday – you and me and Johnny – it was a mistake. It was *my* mistake. It was too early. It was too much to ask of you so soon after losing your dad."

I nodded, and felt a shower of pinpricks – tears rising quickly, filling my eyes.

"I think perhaps it was too much too soon for me as well, actually," Mum said, and she squeezed my hand again.

I wiped away a couple of my tears.

"Oh, Cait. I hate seeing you so angry and so sad."

I nodded, pulling my hand away from hers now to wipe more of the tears from my face.

"I miss Dad so much," I said.

"I know. I know you do. Here…" she said and she got up and grabbed some tissues and passed them over to me. "Use this. Wipe your face."

"Don't you miss him too?" I asked as she sat back down.

"Of course I do. I miss him all the time. He's with me all the time, in here," she said touching her head, "and here too," she said touching her chest. "He'll never truly be gone."

"Really?" I said. "Because it doesn't seem like that to me. We never talk about him, you never say you miss him any more."

"Would you like to talk about him more?" Mum said.

"Yes," I said. "Because I don't want to forget him – I'm scared that maybe I will."

"You won't, Cait! How could you? He was your dad – you'll never forget him."

"But it's really hard if I can't talk to you about him like we used to."

"What do you mean? I hadn't realized that we'd stopped." Mum looked almost confused.

I looked up at her.

"But we have," I said. "We really have."

She looked down suddenly at her hands in her lap, at her wedding ring. She started twisting it round her finger, twisting the band round and round. She did that when she was upset. I knew she did. She did it the whole way through the funeral, and for days at home after that, whenever anyone came over.

"And you think that's because of Johnny?" she said, looking up at me now. "Is that what you're saying?"

I nodded. "Well, yes. I think so."

She nodded back, looking down again.

"Okay," she said. "I guess...I guess I hadn't realized you felt like that...but I can see now why you might, why you do."

I started crying again. It was relief. It felt so good to hear her saying that in some way she understood.

"The thing is, Cait, I think I've accepted that Dad isn't here any more. I think I accepted it a little while ago now. And I didn't feel good about accepting it at first, especially when I could see how much you were still hurting, wishing he was here. But I couldn't fill that hole or make it better. You know, all I wanted to do was make it better for you."

I nodded. I did know.

"But I had to find a way to accept that Dad was gone," Mum said. "So that I could keep living my life, so that I could still be here for you. I couldn't just stop living my life because he wasn't in it any more. Can you understand that? Does that make any sense to you?"

"Yes," I said, and I nodded.

And I thought about Ceri Rees, and what she had written in her letter about being free, living as someone new. It sounded as if she really didn't have anyone after she lost her mum. Her stepdad had been there for her, but it wasn't the same. He was thrown by grieving too. When I lost Dad, I still had Mum. And Mum had me. We had each other. When Ceri lost her mum she didn't have anyone at all.

"New beginnings are okay, you know?" Mum said. "They don't have to be a betrayal of everything that went before."

"Okay," I said, and I thought about Ceri's butterfly tattoo, and what it meant to her to have it with her always, and I nodded, managing a smile through my tears, because I really did understand. For the first time in ages I felt like I could maybe make better sense of things.

Mum passed me another tissue.

"Let's go out for the day," she said. "You and me. Let's do something nice, something fun. What do you say?"

I screwed up my face, wiping my nose now. "I kind of said I'd meet Marko – you know, the boy from next door?" I felt bad.

"Oh great!" Mum said, laughing. "I send Johnny away and you're dumping me for the guy next door!"

I leaned over and grabbed Mum's hand again.

"No! No, I really want us to do something. I'll text him. I can meet him later. There's a BBQ this evening at the beach. I was going to go, if that's okay? I can see him then."

Mum nodded. "You like this Marko then?" she said. "You really like him?"

"Yeah," I said. "I think I do."

And I thought about how Marko made me feel when I was with him. He made me feel happy, like anything in the world was possible when he was close to me. If Johnny made Mum feel like that, or even half as good as that, after everything she'd been through, then I could see that I needed to make the effort with him. Or at least try harder.

I stood up.

"I think I'll go and get dressed and text Marko about meeting later on," I said. I picked up my plate of cold, uneaten toast to go and dump it in the bin.

Mum stood up too. "Sure," she said, taking the plate out of my hand. "Leave that. I'll clear up in here and then go and get myself ready too." And as she walked over to the sink I looked down at her newspaper still sitting on the table, and I saw the headline.

Woman's Body Found at Glan Y Mor Beach.

"Is this about the body they found yesterday?" I said, quickly scooping the paper up off the table, scanning it for news. "Does it say who she is?"

Mum walked over to me.

"Yes, they've confirmed it's not the missing girl," Mum said. "Thank god. Except they still need to find her, bring her home."

I read on, the relief flooding me, turning away from Mum so I could hide the tears that were threatening to fall again.

The body of a woman in her twenties was found yesterday around 6 a.m. by fisherman in the Glan y Mor Beach area. The cause of death is still unknown, but an autopsy will be carried out later this week. An investigation has been opened as to the identity of the woman, who at this stage is unknown to police. Any earlier connection to the case of missing teenager Ceri Rees has now been discounted.

It wasn't Ceri. She was alive. Alys was free.

"But of course it's someone else's poor daughter, mother or sister," Mum said.

"Yes," I said. "I know." And as I put the newspaper back down on the table I thought about Ceri, and I wondered where she was, and if she was okay. I wished there was some way that we could find out – really know – that she was totally okay.

"Do you think they're still coming?" I said looking at Marko.

We were sitting by a fire on the beach in the cove, close to where we'd been sitting at the party the first night I'd met everyone. It was strange to think that was only six days ago. So much had happened in six days. It was all kind of extraordinary when I thought about it now.

"You know, if Hannah got a better offer tonight, a party or something, that's where she'll be," Marko said. "And Ifan may well have gone with her. I don't know. Or he might have decided to stay at home."

I nodded, looking out at the sea. The light was dim, but it hadn't completely faded. The water was bizarrely still, the stillness broken only by the passing gulls and a family throwing a stick for their dog, who was running in and out of the water's edge below.

I felt Marko lean into me. The closeness of him, the sense of his arm, his chest, his body right up next to mine, felt good. I let myself lean back into him, and he lifted his arm up and put it round me and I moved in even closer.

"You cold?" he said.

"No."

"Good."

We sat like that watching the dog bounding across the sand for the stick and then back into the water again, splashing around. So much joy. And yet only yesterday there'd been a body found in these waters further up the coast. It was hard to comprehend.

"I was so relieved this morning when I read about the body they found at Glan y Mor," I said.

"Yeah, me too," Marko said.

"It felt kind of weird though. I mean it's good that they've said it's not Ceri, but we knew that yesterday, didn't we? And meanwhile, her stepdad and the police are still looking for her. She's still missing. We know a lot more than we should."

"But we don't know where she went," Marko said. "I wish we did. It would make it so much easier if we did."

I nodded. "So are you going to go to the police?" I asked. "Have you decided?"

"I haven't stopped thinking about what to do since we

left the hut last night. I've hardly slept thinking about it," Marko said.

I understood how he felt. I'd had all that stuff going on with Mum this morning, but still, thinking about Ceri had stayed with me the whole time too.

"But I've decided that I'm going to do what Ceri asked us to do and what Ifan seems so sure we should do. I'm going to keep Ceri's secret, let Ifan look after her things. I won't go to the police. Not for now, anyway."

I nodded. I was surprised, because Marko had been so sure last night that the right thing to do was to go to the police.

"She has good reason to do what she's done," Marko said. "It can't have been easy for her to do it. She's put her trust in us. Every time I think about what to do I keep coming back to that – trust."

"If we knew where she was," I said looking at him now, "would you change your mind?"

"Yeah," Marko said. "I think I would."

I nodded. I would have done too. It was about knowing she was safe.

"Even if we went to the police now, told them what we know, handed over the letter, her things – none of it would help them find her, and anyway, she's told us she doesn't want to be found."

I nodded. I could see that Marko was still struggling with how he felt – he'd clearly been so torn when we'd all left each other last night – but he was sure now about what he was going to do.

"Do you think Hannah will say anything to anyone?" I asked.

Marko shook his head. "She just wants to know that Alys has gone, that she's not coming back. But you know, I'm doing this partly because I think she will come back – to see Ifan and to get her things. Those things are just too important to her; she won't let them go. I think she'll come back as soon as she can, and then we'll know she's okay. That's what I'm hoping, anyway."

"Alys must have really disturbed Hannah," I said.

"She did. And you know she disturbed me too," Marko said.

"I know I never met her, but I just can't stop thinking about what it must have been like for her to have been in the car that killed her mother and her stepsister, and to have survived. I just can't imagine how it must have felt. I guess I don't think any of us really can."

"You know, that day at the lake, the way she was with us all," Marko said. "It was like she thought she was indestructible. I didn't understand it then, but when I look back, I can see that now."

"I guess all she wanted was to not be the person she was any more," I said. "It was too hard. So she tried turning herself into someone new."

"Yeah," Marko said. "So maybe Hannah wasn't so wrong about her playing with us after all. But I do get it – what she said in her letter about being the one who was left. I mean, who wants to be the one left behind?"

I thought about Mum and me. When Dad died we were the ones left behind. It was different for Ceri, but there was something about what she went through that felt the same.

"I keep asking myself whether she was trying to die that day at the lake to prove some point – to test herself. She said in her letter that she'd survived the crash against all the odds," Marko said. "It was like she was trying to test that again."

"Grief can do strange things to you," I said. "It can make you feel like you have no reason to go on living. It can take away your choices. It can swallow you whole."

"You know, at first I thought that what we did at the lake was thrilling, amazing, but it wasn't – it was frightening. Maybe Ceri really did want to die and somehow meeting us, pretending she was Alys, saved her in some way – maybe we really did pull her through."

I thought about Mum and the conversation we'd had

that morning. I guessed, for her, I was the reason she'd had to go on living. The reason she'd always had was me.

"I just don't understand how Hannah can still be so angry," I said, turning to look at Marko. "Ceri's life was so complicated. That's what made her act like she did at the lake, be like she was with you all. Surely Hannah can see that now?"

"Hannah sees things in this really black and white way, you know? She doesn't do well with grey." He paused for a moment, his eyes on mine. "Not like you," he said.

"Me?" I said, looking away from Marko now, because the way he was looking, how close he was to me, was kind of brilliant but terrifying, and I didn't quite know how to be. "I think I'm still learning," I said, "about everything…"

"Yeah, well, I've just had two of the craziest summers of my life, and I'm still not sure what's been happening or what will happen now," Marko said, softening the moment.

I laughed and looked down at the sand. Was this summer just crazy to him? It had been crazy, what with everything that had happened since I'd arrived, but meeting him had meant, that for me at least, it was other things too.

There was a silence between us.

"I guess Ifan is in the hardest place of all, holding on to Alys's things, waiting for her to come back," Marko said.

"I hope you're right," I said. "I hope she comes back soon."

Marko nodded. "You know, if we don't hear from her or if anything changes – anything at all – and it feels right for me, then I'll go to the police. I'll go against Ifan. I couldn't live with myself if something happened to her."

The fire began to spit and crack. Some wet wood amongst the dry started hissing, making a thin stream of smoke rise before our eyes. We sat and watched it together, and Marko gently took my hand and held it in his.

Neither of us spoke as we watched the light begin to fade, the horizon blurring then disappearing as the gulls performed their final swoops.

"You know I leave in a week," I said.

"I know," he said.

I looked down at our hands, still intertwined.

I really wanted to say something, say everything that I was thinking and feeling in the moment, but it was all a big messy jumble in my head, because all I was thinking about was how good it was to feel Marko's hand in mine, and how happy I was that we were here together, like we were, without Ifan or Hannah, and completely on our own.

I turned to face him, and he turned to face me.

We looked at each other, our eyes scanning each other's faces, and without thinking, we moved towards one other and we kissed – and I felt like I was turning slowly with the world and the world was slowly turning with me. All time slipped and I was elsewhere.

We separated – our foreheads gently tipping against one another.

"We shouldn't do this," I said.

"Why?"

"Because I'll be gone in a week."

"Cait," Marko said, looking at me now. "Let's not think about what happens in a week. Literally anything can happen in a week, right?" he said and he smiled.

"Okay," I said and I smiled too, because I knew exactly what he meant. And I pushed away all thoughts of what would happen when this holiday came to an end, and I thought about what Mum had said about beginnings. Perhaps this could be a beginning.

Who is FAYE BIRD?

Faye lives in London with her family and a large, fluffy ginger cat called Ralph. She studied Philosophy and Literature at Warwick University and always wanted to be a writer, but wasn't brave enough initially to try. Without any idea of what else she might like to do she decided to work in as many different jobs as she could in the hope that she might find one that would feel like a fit. She worked in a toyshop, a field and a theme park before landing a job that she immediately fell in love with in a literary agency. Faye worked her way up from receptionist to agent and represented film and TV screenwriters for over twelve years. Then in 2012, she decided to be brave and commit seriously to her writing.

My Secret Lies with You is Faye's third novel for young adults, following *My Second Life* and *What I Couldn't Tell You*. When she is not writing she works in a primary school supporting children with their reading.

ACKNOWLEDGEMENTS

With thanks to the following people, without who, this book wouldn't be what it is – Hilary Delamere, Jessica Hare at The Agency – crucial first readers; Anne Finnis and Sarah Stewart – brilliant, insightful, thoughtful editors; Jacob Dow and Katarina Jovanovic at Usborne, but in particular Jacob for his passion and commitment to getting this book seen; the whole team at Usborne for turning my words into a book, especially Sarah Cronin and Will Steele for the stunning design inside and out; Helen Greathead for the copy edit and Gareth Collinson and Graham Smith for proofreading; Sue Wallinan for reading an early draft over her Christmas break and supporting the book so beautifully; Sarah J. Harris for her support too, which I hugely appreciate; Sarah Govett, Lucy Noguera, Alison Martino – friends, colleagues and all round supporters; Zanna Bird for being the best friend a girl could ever have; my family for their patience when my head has been in the story; the British Library for the focus and inspiration that comes with my BL writing days.

Also by FAYE BIRD

"utterly gripping"
Anthony McGowan

In my first life
My
Catherine died.
Second
And I think it
Life
was because of me...

Faye Bird

Praise for MY SECOND LIFE

"An astonishingly accomplished debut novel.
Highly recommended."
School Librarian

"The plot is truly compelling, with the tension
ratcheted high."
School Library Journal

"A clever plot, defined characters, and fabulous writing."
Reader review, *The Guardian*

"I was completely gripped throughout the story."
Once Upon A Bookcase

"This debut thriller gets off to a cracking start…"
The Daily Mail

"An ingenious concept, an intriguing mystery and
a gripping story told with pace and passion… "
Blackpool Gazette

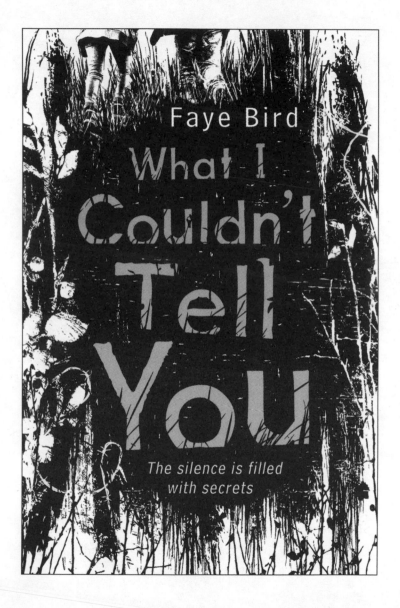

Faye Bird

What I Couldn't Tell You

*The silence is filled
with secrets*

"Faye Bird should be congratulated on giving such rare but accurate insight into the little-known but distressing condition of Selective/Situational Mutism."
Lindsay Whittington, Co-ordinator and Founding Member Selective Mutism Information & Research Association (SMIRA)

"I strongly recommend this book and I'd love to read more by Faye Bird in future."
YA Under My Skin

"This is a truly brilliant book."
A Daydreamer's Thoughts

"It's a really well-judged thriller, (it) does an amazing job of delving into people's emotions, what breaks them and what they do about it…"
Another Teen Reader

"A gripping thriller…"
Rachel Bustin

"A very detailed understanding of the life of a SM young person… YA readers will find a great deal to identify with in the twisting and turning sub-plots."
Awfully Big Reviews

FAYE BIRD shares
some secret thoughts:

Where do your ideas come from?

I'm rather nosy – I think most writers are. So my stories come from observing places and listening to the people and general goings-on around me. With *My Second Life* I was inspired in part by a conversation I had with my son. I wrote *What I Couldn't Tell You* after I heard a girl who had previously suffered with Selective Mutism speaking about her experiences. *My Secret Lies With You* started differently. I spent many of my school holidays with friends in North Wales and I really wanted to try and capture the sense of that place in a story.

You seem to be very interested in characters who have more than one identity. Why do you think that is?

Life can be changeable. And while change can be positive, it can also be hard; it can chip away at what we think we know and in turn who we think we are. I think we all experience times when we feel clear about who we are and times when we don't. Sometimes the person we feel we are privately might be different to the one we present, or are seen to be, publicly. Sometimes the person we think we are is at odds with the person we thought we were to begin with. A first-person narrative really allows you to explore this in a story.

Your novels have a strong emotional core – are you a very emotional person?
I would describe myself as an emotional person in as much as I often feel things very deeply. But I am also quite a private person. I think writing can be a really powerful way to express yourself.

The cliff-jumping incident was based on real experience. Can you tell us about it?
I was on a road trip with friends in the US and up for adventure. But not up for jumping off a cliff into a lake! I remember feeling the pressure of the group to jump. I wanted to be brave. But I couldn't do it. I watched my friends fly off the edge of the rock, heard their screams, and ended up standing alone at the top. I was the only one who didn't jump. One of my friends was horrendously bruised where she hit the water, like Hannah, but she was on a complete high after she jumped. I felt terrible that I hadn't shared in that experience, but the feeling passed, and if you asked me whether I'd make a different choice now, I'm certain that I wouldn't. I'd just be more confident about the fact that I didn't want to jump.

Love this book? Love Usborne YA

Follow us online and sign up to the Usborne YA
newsletter for the latest YA books,
news and competitions:

usborne.com/yanewsletter

 @UsborneYA

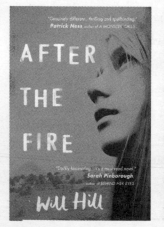